HEROES OF THE WOMEN'S SUFFRAGE MOVEMENT

ELIZABETH BLACKWELL

DOCTOR AND ADVOCATE FOR WOMEN IN MEDICINE

LISA A. CRAYTON

Enslow Publishing
101 W. 23rd Street
Suite 240
New York, NY 10011
USA

enslow.com

Published in 2017 by Enslow Publishing, LLC.
101 W. 23rd Street, Suite 240, New York, NY 10011

Library of Congress Cataloging-in-Publication Data

Names: Crayton, Lisa A., author.
Title: Elizabeth Blackwell : doctor and advocate for women in medicine / Lisa A. Crayton.
Description: New York, NY : Enslow Publishing, 2017. | Series: Heroes of the women's suffrage movement | Includes bibliographical references and index.
Identifiers: LCCN 2016001026 | ISBN 9780766078901 (library bound)
Subjects: LCSH: Blackwell, Elizabeth, 1821-1910—Juvenile literature. | Physicians—New York (State)—Biography. | Women physicians—New York (State)—Biography—Juvenile literature. | Women physicians—England—Biography—Juvenile literature.
Classification: LCC R154.B623 C73 2017 | DDC 610.92—dc23
LC record available at http://lccn.loc.gov/2016001026

Printed in the United States of America

To Our Readers: We have done our best to make sure all websites in this book were active and appropriate when we went to press. However, the author and the publisher have no control over and assume no liability for the material available on those websites or on any websites they may link to. Any comments or suggestions can be sent by e-mail to customerservice@enslow.com.

Photo Credits: Cover, Time Life Pictures/Timepix/The LIFE Picture Collection/Getty Images; cover, interior design elements: wongwean/Shutterstock.com (grunge background on introduction, back cover); Attitude/Shutterstock.com (purple background); Sarunyu_foto/Shutterstock.com (white paper roll); Dragana Jokmanovic/Shutterstock.com (gold background); Eky Studio/Shutterstock.com (grunge background with stripe pattern); macknimal/Shutterstock.com (water color like cloud); Borders-Kmannn/Shutterstock.com (vintage decorative ornament); pp. 5, 12, 21, 67, 85, 95 Library of Congress, Prints and Photographs Division; p. 17 Ann Ronan Pictures/Print Collector/Hulton Archive/Getty Images; p. 19 Culture Club/Hulton Archive/Getty Images; p. 25 Museum of the City of New York/Archive Photos/Getty Images; pp. 26–27 Everett Historical/Shutterstock.com; p. 28 H B Blackwell and Lucy Stone speaking announcement, 1866/Wikipedia Commons; pp. 34–35, 39 Courtesy of the Geneva Historical Society; pp. 42–43, 54 Courtesy of the U.S. National Library of Medicine; p. 47 Barbara Leigh Smith Bodichon/File:A brief summary, in plain language, of the most important laws concerning women, together with a few observations thereon/Wikipedia Commons; p. 51 Museum of the City of New York/Byron Collection/Archive Photos/Getty Images; p. 63 MPI/Archive Photos/Getty Images; p. 69 Private Collection/Bridgeman Images; p. 71 Creator: unknown, From the New England Hospital for Women and Children Records, Sophia Smith Collection, Smith College (Northampton, Massachusetts); p. 75 Al Fenn/The LIFE Picture Collection/Getty Images; p. 79 Joseph Kyle/File:Mott Lucretia Painting Kyle 1841/Wikimedia Commons; p. 89 GraphicaArtis/Archive Photos/Getty Images; p. 92 Transcendental Graphics/Archive Photos/Getty Images; p. 98 Joseph Stanley Kozlowski/File:EBlackwell1905/Wikimedia Commons; p. 103 Private Collection/© Look and Learn/Illustrated Papers Collection/Bridgeman Images; p. 105 Walery/File:Elizabeth Garrett Anderson/Wikimedia Commons; p. 110 NewTestLeper79/File:Elizabeth Blackwell headstone/Wikimedia Commons; p. 114 Galyamin Sergej/Shutterstock.com.

CONTENTS

BLAZING TRAILS

> "I knew that, however insignificant my individual effort might be, it was in the right direction, and in accordance with . . . our [human] race's progress."[1]
> —Elizabeth Blackwell

In the twenty-first century, a woman's role is complicated. On one hand, jobs for women keep increasing. Women today hold positions of influence like never before. They work in many different fields. Some head large companies that earn billions of dollars in profits, while others run small family businesses. Some direct colleges or universities, others lead homeschools. Some women are experts in STEM (science, technology, engineering, and mathematics) fields—others rock the arts. Some serve in military units, others in local police and fire departments. Some guide nonprofit groups, others manage in-home businesses. Some run sports teams, while others are making and breaking records on the field!

Elizabeth Blackwell (1821–1910) was the first woman in the United States to earn a medical degree. Though many stood in her way, Blackwell persevered to attain her goals.

That's hardly a complete list. Women work in a dizzying array of jobs. Women on the combat field? Why not? If a woman desires to make a difference in any arena, she has the right to do so. Girls have the same right. Current social and political climates make all of this possible. However, this was not always the case.

A LIFE OF LIMITATIONS

Elizabeth Blackwell lived in a different time. During most of her life, gender roles were clearly defined and established. Those dictated people's lives. Women and men had specific roles. They performed separate tasks based solely on their sex. This is best seen by looking at women's daily lives of the time. Women were considered "delicate creatures." They were viewed as weaker beings who needed caring for by men, who were considered smarter.

In general, it was believed that women were created to care for home and family. Women's working roles varied based on their family background. This was especially true as the industrial revolution sparked high demand for workers. Many poor women, for example, took jobs in factories.

Blackwell was born into a middle-class household. Women in these families usually did not work outside the home. But when a woman married, her money, property, and other possessions became her husband's. She no longer had control over those assets.

There were very few professional jobs accessible for all women. Women could teach. They quit teaching once they married. The reasoning behind excluding women from certain professions was numerous. Acceptable eighteenth-century notions of middle-class womanhood began and ended with domesticity [home life] . . . middle-class women were restricted to work in the home, cultivating delicate sensibilities and house-womanly skills and virtues.[2]

Meanwhile, the medical field welcomed women, but only as caregivers. Women were not allowed to become doctors, and it was initially difficult for women to become nurses. Opponents of women as physicians were neither scientific nor consistent. They praised women's abilities as nurturers but rejected their competence in medicine. They offered their arguments for female inferiority, vulnerability, and dependence alongside their claims for women's moral superiority [higher morals] and domestic responsibility.[3]

During Elizabeth Blackwell's time, women did not hold positions of authority in communities or in government. In fact, women could not even vote. Such was Elizabeth Blackwell's world. But that world was changing, and so was she. The changing times led her to become a medical pioneer.

FIGHT FOR WOMEN'S RIGHTS

Slavery still existed in the United States at the time when Blackwell was born. But, people were fighting against it. Slavery in England and America sparked women's desires to be active members of society. Women got involved. Many became abolitionists. White women, free black women, and female fugitive slaves fought to end slavery.

They took on other noticeable roles. They soon began advocating for more expanded rights for women. They fought for the right for safer workplaces, shorter workdays, and higher wages. Many became suffragists, a term used for people who supported voting rights for women.

These brave women faced stiff opposition. Men and even other women tried stopping them. They were beaten, put in jail, fined, and faced other forms of humiliation. Yet, they continued protesting. Eventually, their efforts helped women win voting rights—and slaves win freedom.

Women's involvement paved the way for their lives to radically change. Blackwell became a trailblazer in medicine. She exhibited tremendous strength and perseverance, graduating from medical school. She became the first female doctor! Her groundbreaking activities threw open doors for other women in America and in England to receive similar medical education.

However, her legacy extends beyond the medical field. She proved that an "impossible" career does not exist. Thus, she inspires hope for anyone, male or female, who dreams of pursuing a goal that may seem unattainable. Elizabeth Blackwell's example proves that passion, hard work, and tenacity can take one far.

CHAPTER ONE

BIRTH OF A WORLD CHANGER

> "It is a great advantage to have been born one of a large family group of healthy, active children, surrounded by wholesome influences."[1]
> —Elizabeth Blackwell

When Elizabeth Blackwell was born on February 3, 1821, neither her family nor the other residents of her town of Counterslip, England, had any idea how she would change lives. No one could tell by looking at her that she would grow up to be one of the most famous women in the entire world. They could not have guessed she would become the first woman doctor! Blackwell graduated from medical school in 1849, becoming the first woman in America to do so. She went on to receive hands-on training in many areas of medicine. Elizabeth Blackwell worked hard to achieve tremendous success in her chosen career. She worked in America and in England.

Over the years, she helped other women in both countries gain needed courage and training to also become physicians. Blackwell pushed for reforms that made hygiene and sanitation top priorities in health care. As a doctor, she was passionate about making sure poor people had access to health care. She even started medical facilities, including a hospital led by women.

Doctor Blackwell endured many challenges before achieving her goal. Through tenacity and perseverance she continually achieved her goals. Blackwell is considered a pioneer in the research and development of preventive medicine and a voice of reason and education to women by raising the public awareness of proper female hygiene in the United States as well as England.[2]

Before she started training in medicine, she faced doubts. Blackwell prayed for God's help. She recalled, ". . . the despair which had overwhelmed me vanished. All doubt as to the future, all hesitation as to the rightfulness of my purpose, left me, and never in after-life returned."[3]

A LARGE, LOVING FAMILY

Blackwell's faith was rooted in her childhood upbringing. She was the daughter of Samuel and Hannah Blackwell. The young, religious couple married in 1815. They were strongly committed to faith, family, and social justice issues.

In the early years following their marriage, they had four children. First was Anna, born in 1816. She was joined by Marian, two years later, in 1818. Their brother, Samuel Charles, was born soon after and died while a baby. The couple then had daughter Elizabeth. They sometimes called her Bessie.

After Elizabeth, they had another son, but he also died. "My childish remembrances," she wrote, "are chiefly associated with my elder sisters, for being born between two baby brothers, who both died in infancy, I naturally followed my sisters' lead, and was allowed to be their playmate."[4]

Elizabeth Blackwell (left) is photographed as an adult with her younger brother Henry Browne Blackwell (seated, front). Henry's wife, Lucy Stone, another prominent suffragist, stands behind him.

More playmates soon joined the family. The first was a son, born in 1823. He also was named Samuel Charles. Two years later, baby brother Henry Browne was born in 1825. Following him were the rest of the Blackwell siblings. Emily (1826), Ellen (1828), and Howard (1831).

The Blackwells lived in Bristol at No. 1 Wilson Street, a large home boasting fruit trees, flowers, and a walled garden. It was there where Elizabeth and her sisters used a telescope for looking at neighboring homes. One day, desiring for a better view of one of those owned by the Duchess of Beaufort, the girls sought permission from their father to climb up to the roof. Anna penned a note in their names. Their father responded with a humorous poem denying permission.

Keeping with tradition at the time, the household also included several unmarried female relatives. These were aunts to the Blackwell children. Their aunt Barbara was their father's sister. Elizabeth Blackwell remembered her as, ". . . a somewhat stern though upright ruler of my youngest days . . ."[5]

The extended family enjoyed a strong bond. Blackwell felt there were many benefits of being raised in such a household. She wrote in her autobiography, "The natural and healthy discipline which children exercise upon one another, the variety of tastes and talents, the cheerful companionship, even the rivalries, misunderstandings, and reconciliations where free play is given to natural disposition, under wise but not too rigid oversight, form an excellent discipline for after life."[6]

A UNIQUE FAMILY

The Blackwells were strong supporters of social reform. In England, and later in America, they worked to end slavery and to promote suffrage, education reform, and equal rights for women.[7] Samuel and Hannah Blackwell also were deeply religious. They raised their children in a household where religion played a key role. For them, that included attending Bridge Street Congregational Church. It was part of a Christian denomination focusing on high moral standards and personal responsibility. They took their children regularly.

The family's faith conflicted with the state religion known as Anglicanism, also known as the Church of England. Because the Blackwells did not follow Anglicanism, they were considered "Dissenters" and subject to many social restrictions. They also were blocked from attending certain schools and working in some occupations. Despite those restrictions, the Blackwells enjoyed a happy, full family life.

Like their religious beliefs, Samuel and Hannah Blackwell's parenting style set them apart from other families. Indeed, it was a radical parenting style for the nineteenth century, which greatly influenced their children's futures. They raised their children to treat all people as equals, just as the Bible taught. That is why they raised their sons and daughters the same way. For example, they let their daughters learn the same subjects as their sons. At the time, boys were taught Latin, math, astronomy, and other topics designed to help them become social and political leaders. Most girls received training designed to make them efficient wives. Many did not receive formal education.

Blackwell's parents also let all of their children run and play and act in ways common to children today, but very unique for their time. They believed exercise contributed to good health. Years later, Blackwell would share the same information in a lecture on girls' health. Despite the convention of the time for girls to be quiet, passive, and restrained, her parents encouraged vigorous physical exercise. The children also walked and played outside in their garden. Their governess took them for walks into town and across the countryside.[8]

Samuel Blackwell owned a sugar refinery. Elizabeth called it his sugar-house, recalling how he used to wear a white flannel suit while working. It stuck out in her mind possibly because the refinery was heated. Flannel is normally worn in cold temperatures. The refinery processed sugar cane for use in other foods. It was a thriving business. Income from the business enabled the family to live a good, middle-class lifestyle.

They had a governess to help with the children, had servants for handling various chores, and hired in-home tutors for educating the children in various subjects. Elizabeth spent a happy childhood with her family in England, summering in the country and thriving in a busy household, where social reform was the topic of dinner conversation.[9] She and her siblings discovered the joy of reading, and spent their pocket change mainly on books.

Life began to change. First, a fire destroyed the refinery. Fires in such businesses were common. That did not make them any easier to bear. Samuel lost a substantial portion of his wealth. Around the same time, he experienced losses tied to investments abroad. He pushed on, buying a refinery connected to a home on Nelson Street. The buildings shared a courtyard. Blackwell remembered enjoying "eight very happy years" there.

Those happy years abruptly came to an end when situations in England forced the family's move to America. Violent riots in Bristol broke out as workers protested losses in jobs and wages. Cholera and other diseases raged in England. Cholera is a bacterial disease that causes several symptoms, the worst of which are diarrhea and dehydration. It is spread through filthy water and other unsanitary conditions. It can kill within hours if not properly treated.

Cholera is treatable today. Back then, doctors did not fully understand the disease. They did not

A COURT FOR KING CHOLERA.

This illustration depicts the crowded, unsanitary conditions in London slums. Such conditions led to a cholera epidemic in England. This panic, along with the Bristol riots, convinced Elizabeth's father to move his family to America.

have the proper medical equipment to detect it. They did not understand much about it. They also had a difficult time controlling it because of the way the illness spreads, especially in crowded living environments. Many people died from the disease.

These situations prompted the Blackwells' decision to relocate to America. Moving day finally came in August 1832. The Blackwell entourage included a total of fifteen people: eight children, several aunts, and the servants. They anticipated enjoying a lifestyle similar to the one they had in

America. They traveled by ship on the *Cosmo.* The trip took about seven weeks.

The *Cosmo* carried over two hundred passengers. A passenger's experience while traveling by sea depended on how much or little they could afford for their passage. Families like the Blackwells had first-class tickets. They enjoyed better conditions and other advantages, although the space was still cramped. Elizabeth suffered from seasickness during the trip, but otherwise the Blackwells enjoyed relatively good health on board.

This contrasted with the conditions below deck. Poorer people traveled in steerage, a less desirable section of the ship saved for people who paid the lowest fares. It was a deck area usually reserved for cargo. During the trip to the United States, cholera broke out in this area. Several steerage passengers died.

LIFE IN NEW YORK CITY

After the journey ended, The Blackwells settled in New York City. Soon after, they welcomed another baby boy to their family. They named him George Washington Blackwell. New York City offered the family a chance to get involved in religious activities. The children had opportunities to attend school. The family quickly also got involved in the slave resistance movement and began to attend abolitionist meetings.

They associated with well-known resistance leaders, including Dr. Lyman Beecher. The minister was known for his sermons on antislavery topics. His daughter was Harriet Beecher Stowe. The Beecher family moved to Cincinnati, Ohio, in 1832 and became greatly involved in the resistance movement. Stowe became an abolitionist involved in the underground railroad in Ripley, Ohio. Ripley was a busy stop on the underground railroad. The "conductors" there helped thousands of fugitive slaves escape to freedom. Stowe associated with some of those abolitionists, including Levi Coffin and John Rankin. She later became known for writing *Uncle Tom's Cabin.* She believed that many people did not have firsthand experience witnessing slavery. She wanted to open their eyes to the truth.

In America, the Blackwells associated with abolitionist Dr. Lyman Beecher (center), his daughter Harriet Beecher Stowe, and son Henry Ward Beecher.

The Blackwells also met William Lloyd Garrison. Garrison was the publisher of *The Liberator.* The paper was the main voice for antislavery reform for nearly thirty-five

WILLIAM LLOYD GARRISON (1805-1879)

William Lloyd Garrison was born into a poor white family in Newburyport, Massachusetts. He grew up doing odd jobs. He trained as an apprentice in several fields, including journalism. It became his life's work. Garrison worked for several newspapers. He learned essential writing and editing skills.

He became an antislavery supporter through his work at one newspaper. He believed people's hearts could be changed by persuasion, or "moral suasion." He became a newspaper publisher in hopes of changing people's hearts and minds about slavery.

Garrison is most remembered and celebrated for the *Liberator.* He published the weekly newspaper in New York City from 1831–1865. It loudly protested the cruelties of slavery. In the face of constant opposition, he kept publishing the paper. He believed that ending slavery was more important than his being politically correct for the times. Once slavery ended, he felt his paper had fulfilled its purpose, and he shut down the paper.

Garrison met the Blackwells once they moved to New York City and became active in the resistance movement. Elizabeth Blackwell had fond childhood memories of him.

years. Garrison visited the Blackwells' home on different occasions. Elizabeth remembered him as an adult who loved children. In turn, the children enjoyed hearing him recite Russian poetry.

Among the other influential reformers the Blackwells met in America was *Liberator* publisher William Lloyd Garrison, a powerful antislavery voice.

UNEXPECTED TRAGEDY

The Blackwells' antislavery views conflicted with their business interests. Samuel Blackwell owned a sugar refinery in New York City. The challenge: most sugar cane was harvested by slaves. That was a problem for him. As an abolitionist, he wanted slavery to end. To him, using a product that involved slave labor was a way of helping slavery thrive. He decided to stop using it. He tried refining sugar from beets. He could not master the process. Eventually, his business failed.

In 1837, New York City experienced a depression. The economic downturn further crunched the family's finances. Their situation was bleak. Samuel and Hannah chose moving again as a means of hopefully rebuilding their family's finances. In May 1838, when Elizabeth was seventeen years old, the family moved to Cincinnati, Ohio. Their friends Dr. Lyman Beecher and his family had moved there years before and were active antislavery supporters.

Cincinnati was a small town, but the family had big hopes. Anna and Marian did not come along. The family also could not afford to bring their servants. Only one aunt made the trip. The family enjoyed watching the scenery unfold as they drew closer to their new hometown.

Samuel had moved as a business opportunity arose, allowing for his business expansion. He hoped for a new beginning, with restored financial wealth and diminished money problems. Initially, the family enjoyed getting to know the West, which was very different from the East.

Tragedy struck, however. Samuel Blackwell fell ill not long after they moved to the city. He died in August. It was a shocking blow to the family's high hopes. Blackwell recalled: "The irreparable loss completely altered our lives. Recovering from the first effects of the stunning blow, we began to realise our position, and the heavy responsibilities henceforth developing on us."[10]

CHAPTER TWO

ROAD LESS TRAVELED

> "... I soon felt the want of a more engrossing pursuit than the study of music, German, and metaphysics...."[1]
> —Elizabeth Blackwell

Samuel Blackwell's death in 1838 shook his family. They never expected this tragedy, and they were absolutely unprepared for it. When Blackwell died, he left his family with very little money, in an unfamiliar city where they knew few people. After burying their father, the Blackwell children realized something had to be done.

The family brainstormed ways to bring money into their home. The three oldest girls, Anna, Marian, and Elizabeth, started a private boarding school for girls in their home in 1838. Their brother Samuel worked at the Cincinnati Court House. Together, they managed to support the family until the rest of their siblings could also work and bring in needed money. They paid bills, bought food, and spent their salaries on anything else the family needed.

As more siblings started working, the family's plight improved. The children pooled their monies, pulling their family out of debt. Around this time, the eldest three Blackwell sisters became more aware of "new views of social and religious duty in the untrammeled [unrestrained] atmosphere of the West."[2]

Elizabeth Blackwell wrote, "The wider education of women was a subject then coming to the front; and we three sisters threw ourselves with ardour [sic] into the public conferences held in Cincinnati on this subject. . . ."[3] They joined the Episcopal Church. They became involved in political activities, attending conventions and public meetings.

In 1842, they closed the boarding school. Elizabeth took on private students to keep busy and earn money. She received an invitation to head a girl's school in Henderson, Kentucky. She accepted because of the expected salary.

It took four days to get to Henderson by boat. Her excitement turned to disappointment when she arrived. The town's appearance did not meet her expectations. The school was not ready for use. Worse, she wrote, "The region of Kentucky . . . was a tobacco-growing district. I there gained my first practical experience of negro slavery and the crude civilization of a Western slave state."[4]

It was a wake-up call for the antislavery supporter. She had never seen slavery up close, or the

After her father's sudden death, Elizabeth Blackwell and her sisters opened a boarding school for girls. And so began Blackwell's dedication to the education of women, despite society's restrictions.

ways in which it affected slaves and owners. It was worse than she ever imagined. She hated how masters treated slaves. One day a slave girl was placed as a human shield between Blackwell and a too-hot fire. That bothered Blackwell. Concerning her overall feelings, she wrote:

> I dislike slavery more and more every day: I suppose I see it here in its mildest form. . . . But to live in the midst of beings degraded to the utmost in body and mind, drudging on from earliest morning to latest night, cuffed about by everyone, scolded at all day long, blamed unjustly, and . . . with no hope for the future . . . to live in their midst, utterly unable to help them, is to me dreadful. . . .[5]

As she moved farther away from New York City, Blackwell witnessed the evils of the institution she had been fighting. In Kentucky, the abolitionist saw slavery firsthand, and she never forgot the anger she felt from the injustice.

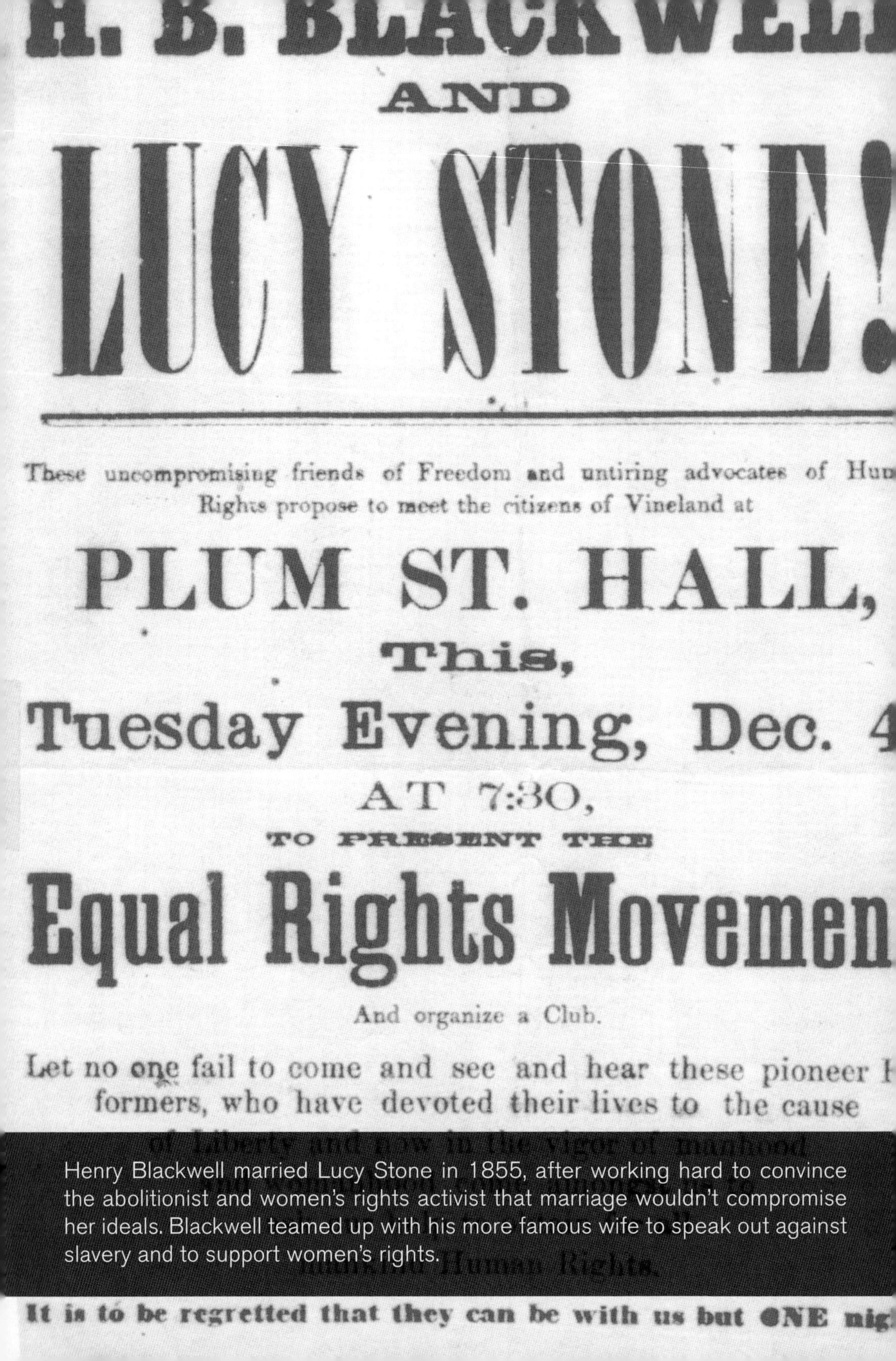

Henry Blackwell married Lucy Stone in 1855, after working hard to convince the abolitionist and women's rights activist that marriage wouldn't compromise her ideals. Blackwell teamed up with his more famous wife to speak out against slavery and to support women's rights.

RETURN TO CINCINNATI

At the end of her teaching contract, Blackwell left Henderson. She returned home. Her family had moved to the Walnut Hills suburb of Cincinnati. It was near the Lane Theological Seminary, run by the Beechers. Harriet Beecher had since married Calvin Stowe, a professor at the ministry training school. Around this time, Elizabeth's brother, Henry, married Lucy Stone. The Blackwell family thrived in Walnut Hills. Elizabeth did not work, but leisurely enjoyed studying various subjects. Soon, however, boredom overtook her. She wanted something meaningful to do.

INSPIRED WORDS

In 1845, Elizabeth Blackwell received a push in the right direction regarding her future while visiting a friend one day. Mary Donaldson had cancer. She mentioned to Blackwell her feelings about the care she received from male doctors. She concluded, "You are fond of study, have health and leisure; why not study medicine?"[7]

Blackwell considered the idea preposterous. Women could not be doctors! She could recall at least three situations while growing up that proved she would not make a good one. Being sick made her feel "foolishly ashamed." Once she had a fever

LUCY STONE (AUGUST 13, 1818-OCTOBER 19, 1893)

From an early age, Lucy Stone believed women should have more rights. She felt they should have the right to vote, attend school, and own property. She taught school, sold products, and did other work to pay for attending Oberlin College. She graduated in 1847 at almost thirty years old.

She was an abolitionist and believed in suffrage. She advocated for the end of slavery. She delivered speeches on women's rights and helped in other ways. By the 1850s, Lucy Stone was one of the most famous women in the United States. Success as an antislavery lecturer in the 1840s had reinforced her personal commitment to what she capitalized as "The Cause." At first, Lucy meant that this was about the abolitionist efforts ". . . [b]ut to the chagrin of antislavery leaders . . . Lucy increasingly inserted stories about the women's plight in her speeches."[6]

Despite opposition to her inclusion of women's rights issues, she kept giving speeches to help advance those anyway. She died in 1893. She was seventy-five years old. She had spent nearly two-thirds of her life committed to the women's rights movement.

and chills and tried unsuccessfully to walk it off, rather than resting. When that failed she shut herself up in a dark room. On occasions, she tried to toughen her body by sleeping on the floor. She tried fasting from foods for a couple of days. None of these things worked.

Blood and body parts also made her nauseous. One day she was repulsed in a class when her teacher brought in an animal's eyeball to discuss as part of the lesson. Just thinking about it made her squeamish. A career in medicine did not seem possible given these factors.

Other things hinted at the possibility, however. She did not plan on marrying. She was easily bored by social activities that did not tax her intellect. Her family did not need her to work to support them. The more she thought about it, the more she liked the idea. She decided to follow her friend's advice. Unfortunately, she did not know how to become a doctor, or what education was needed. Seeking to gain information and also to test her idea, Blackwell wrote letters to doctors she knew for their opinions.

She recalled, "The answers I received were curiously unanimous. They all replied to the effect that the idea was a good one, but that it was impossible to accomplish it; that there was no way of obtaining such an education for a woman . . . and that, in short, the idea, though a valuable one, was impossible of execution."[8]

Friends like Harriet Beecher Stowe also thought the idea was impractical. Rather than alter Blackwell's plans, the responses fueled her desire even more. She shared her idea with other people. She considered all opinions. In the end, she decided to go for her dream. One friend had promised to help fund Blackwell's education. But, in the end, she only offered to loan Blackwell one hundred dollars. Blackwell needed at least $3000 for her educational expenses.

FIRST TRAINING GROUNDS

Hoping to save money for medical school, Blackwell accepted a music teacher's position in Asheville, North Carolina. The school's principal, Reverend John Dickson, was a former doctor. Blackwell hoped to begin studying medicine with him during her off hours. Her family supported her plans. In June 1845, two of her brothers drove her to North Carolina, a trip lasting eleven days. The evening she arrived, she recalled feeling a mix of dread and doubt. After praying, Blackwell no longer doubted her purpose. She felt more confident about the future, knowing her goal was attainable.

Blackwell worked in Asheville for only about six months. Reverend Dickson's school closed, causing her to find another job. She moved to Charleston, South Carolina, in January 1846. She soon accepted a music teacher position at a boarding school. She worked there less than eighteen months. In her spare time, she studied medicine with Dr. Samuel H. Dickson. A doctor and a professor at the local medical college, he was Reverend Dickson's brother. She also learned Greek.

Having lived in Kentucky and Asheville, Blackwell had seen slavery. However, her experiences in Charleston were up close and personal encounters with the disturbing realities of slavery. On more than one occasion she felt indignation at the way slaves were treated. She also felt helpless to speak up. She knew doing so would cause more trouble for slaves.

Blackwell continued saving money. By July 1847, she felt she had enough to pay for medical school. She left Charleston, moving to Philadelphia as it was considered *the* heart of medical training in America. She stayed with a local doctor. She took private anatomy classes with a different doctor. She was grateful for the way he approached the subject. He helped her appreciate the beauty of the body, how it is made and how it functions.

For months, Blackwell lived with a doctor and his family while applying to schools and interviewing with professors. Meanwhile, she attended lectures by another physician, Dr. Joseph Warrington. He also allowed her to visit his patients and use his medical library. Dr. Warrington also spoke with friends about Blackwell's goal.

Each school in Philadelphia had the same answer: No. Some rejection letters were nice; others rudely criticized her for considering such a novel career path for a woman. She received lots of mixed advice. It was suggested that she study abroad in Paris. Someone else suggested the city was too sinful for her to study there as a female and suggested she pretend to be a man. Blackwell wrote, "[N]either the advice to go to Paris nor the suggestion of disguise tempted me for a moment. It was to my mind a moral crusade on which I had entered, a course of justice and common sense, and it must be pursued in the light of day, and with public sanction, in order to accomplish its end."[9]

Blackwell broadened her vision. She applied to other schools throughout the United States. All told, she applied to nearly twenty-nine schools. Being a woman was but one of the challenges she faced. Another was the competitive nature of the medical field. Men saw her as a person who could steal their patients once she became a doctor.

Finally, Geneva Medical College in upstate New York accepted her for admission. Blackwell was ecstatic. Only later did she learn that the male

After receiving discouraging rejections from twenty-nine medical schools, Blackwell heard the only news that mattered: Geneva Medical College in New York State had accepted her into their ranks.

students had voted to let her in only because they thought it was a joke by either Geneva's administration or another school.

LIFE AT SCHOOL

Within a couple days of receiving Geneva Medical College's response, Blackwell headed to New York on November 4. Two of her brothers drove her to the school. Travelling throughout the night, they arrived at 11 p.m. on November 6. The next morning she had her interview with the school and was added to the list as student No. 130. She found a room in a boarding house on the same street as the school, a three-minute walk along a beautiful bank overlooking the lake.

Geneva's male students were shocked when she arrived that day. Because they had considered her application for admission a hoax, they never expected to see her. Prior to her arrival, the group was known for their rowdiness and their noisy behavior during lectures. From the moment she stepped into class that changed. They quickly got used to her presence in the classroom.

Residents of the city were slower to get used to her. Many disapproved of her studies. Some thought she had low morals, while others just believed she had a mental illness. Eventually, however, they accepted her in the community.

Meanwhile at school, Blackwell was enjoying her studies. At first, she was blocked from attending anatomy sessions about the reproductive system. The professor, Dr. James Webster, supported her attendance at the school. However, he thought his jokes might shock her. Blackwell stuck up for her right to attend. She wrote to him, saying that she wanted to be treated like every other student, without restrictions placed on her attendance. Dr. Webster read the letter to the class. She listened nearby. When she heard the clapping, Blackwell rejoiced. She entered the classroom and took her seat. That first session she sat in, the male students laughed and joked. Blackwell pretended their antics did not bother her. She was not embarrassed by the subject matter, and found it fascinating.

TRAINING DURING COLLEGE BREAK

Geneva Medical School's semester ended in January 1848. The break between semesters usually lasted until the fall. In between, students took internships at medical facilities to further their training. The up-close training provided real-world experience identifying illnesses, treating patients, and working with established doctors. The school's male students, like male students at other medical schools, had no difficulty finding places to train.

Blackwell was not as lucky. No facility wanted a female medical school student. She returned to

Philadelphia and taught music lessons for a couple of months. She applied to Blockley Almshouse in Philadelphia. The hospital specialized in treating poor patients, many who were mentally ill. She got the job, working and living on the grounds from roughly March to September.

Young male doctors at the hospital did not want to work with Blackwell. They walked out of rooms when she came in. They did not leave important patient information, so Blackwell had to take extra time learning what ailed patients. The lack of paperwork was a petty act and frustrating to deal with.

Blackwell did not let the young doctors' behavior stop her from learning as much as she could. Despite their chilly reception, Blackwell gained extensive experience and knowledge in various fields of medicine, including in contagious diseases. She returned to Geneva Medical College in October to complete her academic training.

A LADY DOCTOR

Commencement finally arrived on January 23, 1849. While Blackwell's male peers paraded to the ceremony, she sat with her brother at the church. She believed it was more ladylike to sit out the parade. Once the male students received their diplomas, Blackwell went up to receive hers from the school's president, Dr. Hale. "Sir," she said, "I thank you; by the help of the Most High it shall be

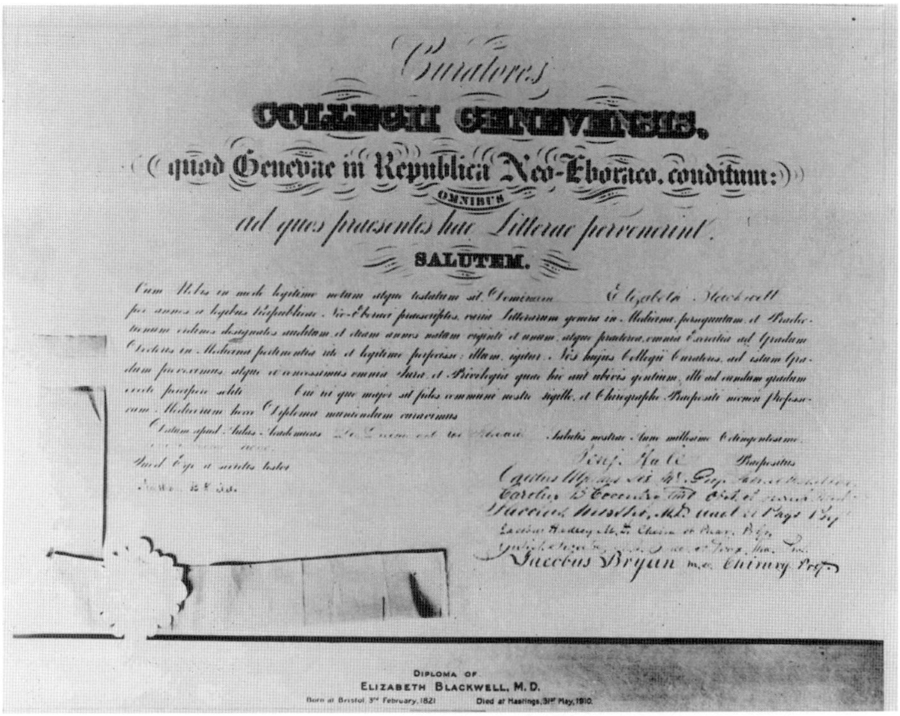

In 1849, Elizabeth Blackwell was awarded a diploma from Geneva Medical School. Although it was a triumphant moment, it didn't mean that things would come easy. Blackwell still had many doors closed to her.

the effort of my life to shed honour [sic] upon your diploma."[10]

Earning a medical degree was just the first hurdle Blackwell had to jump before becoming a career doctor. The next was finding work. She went back to Philadelphia for a short time while seeking employment. She encountered much of the same resistance as she did while looking for an internship during school. No facility wanted to hire a woman doctor.

As she considered options, a cousin visiting America invited her to travel back to England with him. She agreed. In addition to *needing* a job, she believed Europe offered more opportunities for women to study. Before she left America, she became a citizen. She also made a brief stop in Cincinnati to visit her family before meeting up with her cousin in Boston. On April 18, 1849, they sailed to England.

CHAPTER THREE

COMPASSIONATE CARE

> "I must accomplish my end. I consider it the noblest and most useful path that I can tread, and if one country rejects me I will go to another."[1]
> —Elizabeth Blackwell

Blackwell enjoyed social life in London for three weeks. It was a busy time. She visited family, went sightseeing, met with doctors, and visited hospitals. As her visit wrapped up, she headed to Paris. She wrote, "All my teachers and medical friends in America had strongly advised my going to Paris as the one place where I should be able to find unlimited opportunities for study in any branch of medical art. Being then desirous of pursuing surgery as well as medicine, I followed their advice."[2]

She arrived in Paris on May 21, 1849. She found a boarding house to live. Rather than unlimited opportunities, Blackwell encountered the same resistance to female doctors she had experienced in America. Worse, her degree was not honored.

Not speaking fluent French was another strike against her. Acting on advice from doctors, she applied to work at La Maternité. The large hospital provided care to pregnant women before and after they gave birth. It had a reputation as the best school in the world for students to be trained as midwives.

La Maternité did not want a female doctor, but it welcomed Blackwell to come study along with interns learning midwifery. Although disappointed, she accepted an appointment to work at the hospital for three months. She started working at La Maternité in June 1849. The hospital strictly regulated its workers, including their social activities. Blackwell likened it to be being imprisoned when writing to her sister, Marian. Nonetheless, during her three months there she gained valuable experience. She learned many things about the special needs of female patients and infants. She came to appreciate the special health concerns women face. After her first internship ended, Blackwell signed up for three additional months at La Maternité.

Blackwell was disappointed to find that Paris welcomed her ambitions no more than America had. She had to settle for a short term at La Maternité hospital, where she obtained practical experience with female patients.

EYE INFECTION

All along, Blackwell planned on one day becoming a surgeon. Ten months after graduating medical school, her plans were derailed by a freak incident at La Maternité. On November 4, Blackwell was tending to an infant who had a contagious infection called ophthalmia. Pus from the infection splattered, popping into Blackwell's left eye. It became infected. For three weeks, she suffered with both eyes swollen. The hospital granted her sister Anna permission to assist in nursing. Blackwell's condition improved enough for her to leave the hospital. She did so on November 26 with no vision in her left eye and a slightly improved right eye.

For the next six months, Blackwell's recovery was slow. Her eye required continued treatment. From June through August 1850, Blackwell received a special type of water treatment for her eye. She traveled to Gräfenberg for it. The city in the Czech Republic was known for its water cures. The fresh air, long walks, and limited diet helped Blackwell feel much better overall. However, the hydrotherapy did not work. It became clear that the infected left eye would never recover.

Once her eye became painfully inflamed, it needed more attention. Blackwell returned to Paris for treatment by a famous eye doctor. He removed her infected, sightless left eye, replacing it with a glass eye. The procedure was necessary to save

EARLY MEDICAL CARE

Blackwell believed she received excellent health care from the doctor who removed her eye. Yet, in many ways, practicing medicine in the nineteenth century was a guessing game. Doctors did not have many tools commonly used today. Doctors used very basic methods to diagnose disease. Then they used very crude methods to treat them. Some of those involved letting a patient bleed by cutting the skin or using creatures called leeches to suck the blood. Doctors also used instruments that often did more harm than good. In many cases, the cure was worse than the ailment!

Many doctors often made patients' conditions worse due to poor hygiene. There were no guidelines about keeping hands clean. Elizabeth Blackwell learned about the benefits of hygiene and proper sanitation as health tools from her friend Florence Nightingale. Nightingale was a famous nurse whose medical skills and compassionate care made her legendary.

Blackwell became an advocate for teaching patients how to stay healthy by using these basic preventative methods. She advocated that doctors use better sanitary practices. In many ways, her insistence for improvements became essential to transforming the medical field–and to saving patients' lives.

her right eye, and remaining vision. However, it ended Blackwell's dream of becoming a surgeon. She could not perform the delicate work of a surgeon with only one eye. It was a disappointing setback. Yet, it did not stop Blackwell from pursuing other opportunities in medicine.

WORKING IN LONDON

While she recovered from the eye operation, Blackwell's cousin Kenyon Blackwell helped her gain a position to study at St. Bartholomew's Hospital in London. She was overjoyed at the idea of returning to work, especially for one of the city's top hospitals. She left Paris for London.

Blackwell started working at St. Bartholomew's in October 1850. She looked forward to learning "considerably more" about medicine, as the admitting committee had granted her permission to work in any department that welcomed her assistance. Ironically, the only department that blocked her access was the one for female diseases.

Blackwell spent hours each day at the hospital. She visited wards and attended lectures. She was very busy, yet lonely. Her social life picked up when she met two sisters, Anna Leigh Smith and Barbara Leigh Smith, and their friend Bessie Rayner Parkes. Blackwell enjoyed their company and social gatherings. They were active in the women's rights movement. Blackwell became

A BRIEF SUMMARY,

IN PLAIN LANGUAGE,

OF

THE MOST IMPORTANT

LAWS CONCERNING WOMEN;

TOGETHER WITH

A FEW OBSERVATIONS THEREON.

By Barbara Leigh Smith

LONDON:

JOHN CHAPMAN, 8, KING WILLIAM STREET, STRAND.

1854.

In London, Blackwell met women's rights activist Barbara Leigh Smith. Smith's 1854 pamphlet was written in language that could be understood by all classes, and as such was widely circulated and influential as early feminist propaganda.

familiar with the issues. She read about the activities at the Women's Right's Convention in 1850, held in Worcester, Massachusetts.

Blackwell understood why women resisted society's restrictions. She agreed that women needed more rights. She did not agree on the method many reformers proposed for getting those rights. She wrote home about the information she learned about the convention. She noted, "They show great energy, much right feelings, but not to my judgement, a great amount of strong, clear thought. . . . I cannot sympathise [sic] fully with an anti-man movement. I have had too much kindness, aid, and just recognition from men to make such attitude of women otherwise than painful; and I think the true end of freedom may be gained better in another way."[3]

FINDING SOLUTIONS

Blackwell began to question some of the treatments, and she wanted to find other ways of practicing medicine. She studied alternative medical practices. She shared her growing dissatisfaction with her sister Emily. She wrote, "I shall commence as soon as possible building up a hospital in which I can experiment; and the very instant I feel *sure* of any improvement I shall adopt it in my practice, in spite of a whole legion of opponents."[4]

By 1851, Blackwell had gained enough experience at St. Bart's and was ready to open a medical facility. She decided to return to America to do so.

BACK TO AMERICA

Blackwell left England bound for New York City on Saturday, July 26, 1851. She traveled by train, then boarded a ship. She was ready to return to the country that initially closed medical doors to her. Excited about leaving England, she considered it, "Another most important page in life fairly closed."[5] As it closed, another opened, ready to be filled with adventures providing compassionate medical care.

Blackwell was ready to begin her career. New York City was not ready for her. She struggled for years trying to succeed there. She wrote, "The first seven years of New York life were years of very difficult, though steady, uphill work.[6]

She faced several challenges. She needed an affordable place for her practice, patients, and associations with fellow doctors. Doors were closed to her because of her gender—again. Landlords did not want to rent to a woman doctor. Eventually, she located one willing to rent her space—at a steep price—on University Place, in the Greenwich Village section of the city.

Finding patients was not easy. Her practice grew slowly as patients trickled in. Equally challenging was her unmet desire for professional connections. Male doctors did not want to associate with her. This severely hindered her ability to learn from, and share concerns with, more experienced physicians. All of these challenges made being a doctor a lonely career.

Blackwell faced other issues. She occasionally received rude letters from people venting about her being a doctor. She also worried constantly about finances. The first she could do nothing about. The second she tried to change by applying for a job. She still had her medical office, but without patients she had the time to work elsewhere.

She applied for a position as doctor in a dispensary. A dispensary was a medical facility that served primarily poor people. It offered medical treatment and prescriptions. In most instances, medical care was free or very low-cost. This attracted increasing numbers of patients who needed to see a physician but could not afford pricier medical care.

Medical dispensaries, like New York City's Harlem Dispensary, shown above, were places where the poor and indigent could be treated. Blackwell believed such a dispensary would accept her on staff.

The combination of large caseloads and multiple illnesses seen made a dispensary an ideal workplace for doctors like Blackwell, who wanted to quickly expand their medical knowledge. The job she applied for required working in the women's department in a large dispensary. Despite her qualifications, she did not get the job. However, she was advised to start her own dispensary. She later followed that advice and opened one.

POWER-PACKED WORDS

Around this time, medical lectures were popular. They provided information in a social setting. People liked listening to doctors give lectures. Those special speeches focused on health topics. They showcased a doctor's medical knowledge, while often attracting more clients to his practice over time. Like her male counterparts, Blackwell began giving lectures.

With a struggling practice, Blackwell had the free time to develop some of these. In the spring of 1852, she delivered the first six. They made up a series about health issues girls face. The lectures drew from her medical knowledge, but they also included information she learned from experience.

She shared her views about the connection between girls' health and exercise. She believed exercise built strong bodies. She had been an active girl, thanks to her father's progressive views.

She encouraged listeners to equip themselves with knowledge needed to build up girls' minds concerning their bodies. Teaching girls about their bodies would be a gift that served them for a lifetime, she believed. These lectures, owing to the social and professional connections that resulted from them, gave [Blackwell her] first start in practical medical life.[7]

A small group of women attended the lectures held in a basement classroom used for Sunday school. Some were Quakers. Over time, they became her patients—and friends. She later noted, ". . . my practice during those early years became very much a Quaker practice; and the institutions which sprang up later owed their foundation to the active support of this valuable section of the community."[8]

Stacy B. Collins was an influential Quaker who hired Blackwell as his family's physician. Blackwell had the pleasure of serving three generations of the family. Many years later, one of his female relatives became a doctor. Blackwell fondly called Dr. Mary B. Hussey "her first baby." The endearing phrase referred to either the fact that Blackwell attended the baby's birth, or started treating Mary when she was an infant. Either way, having a female doctor as a family physician likely inspired Mary's career goal. Blackwell's influence on the women in medicine was continuing.

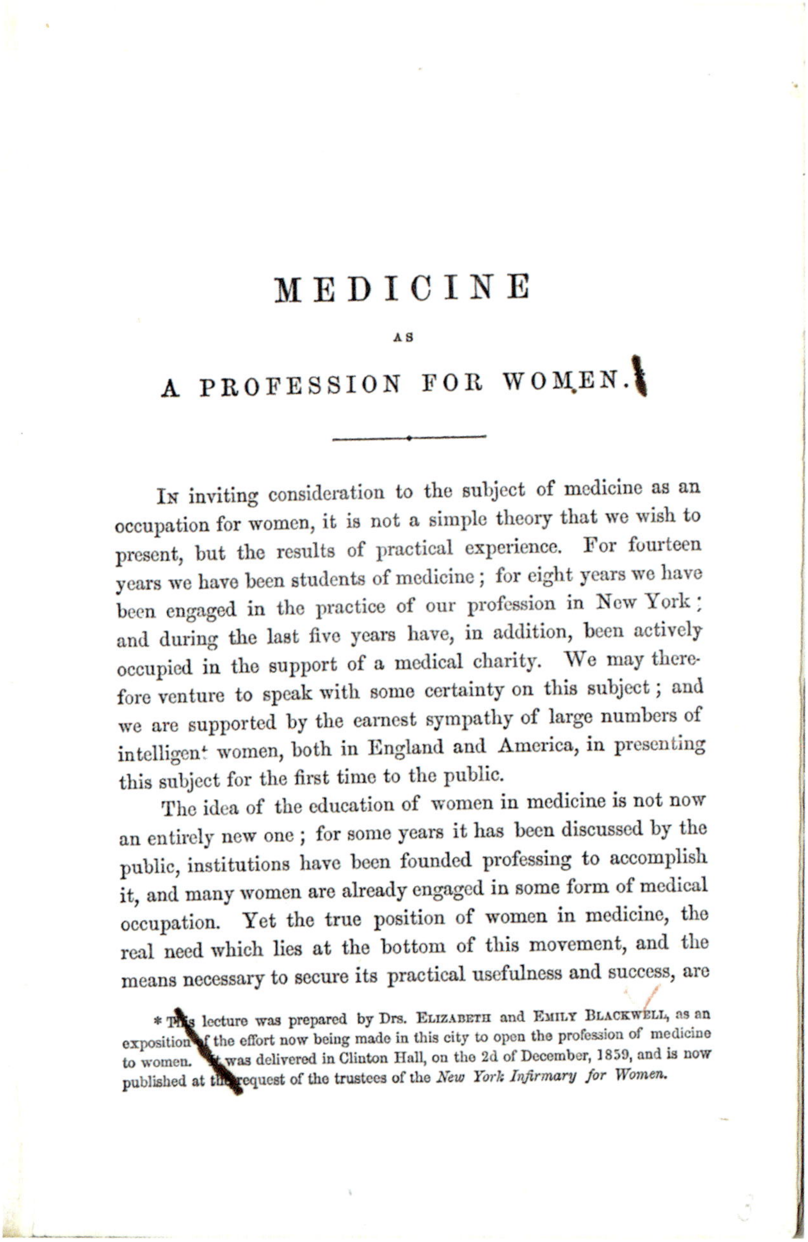

MEDICINE

AS

A PROFESSION FOR WOMEN.*

In inviting consideration to the subject of medicine as an occupation for women, it is not a simple theory that we wish to present, but the results of practical experience. For fourteen years we have been students of medicine; for eight years we have been engaged in the practice of our profession in New York; and during the last five years have, in addition, been actively occupied in the support of a medical charity. We may therefore venture to speak with some certainty on this subject; and we are supported by the earnest sympathy of large numbers of intelligent women, both in England and America, in presenting this subject for the first time to the public.

The idea of the education of women in medicine is not now an entirely new one; for some years it has been discussed by the public, institutions have been founded professing to accomplish it, and many women are already engaged in some form of medical occupation. Yet the true position of women in medicine, the real need which lies at the bottom of this movement, and the means necessary to secure its practical usefulness and success, are

* This lecture was prepared by Drs. Elizabeth and Emily Blackwell, as an exposition of the effort now being made in this city to open the profession of medicine to women. It was delivered in Clinton Hall, on the 2d of December, 1859, and is now published at the request of the trustees of the *New York Infirmary for Women.*

While Blackwell struggled to practice medicine, she found success as a lecturer. Blackwell published her lectures, bringing attention to her name and her cause. This published lecture was delivered by Elizabeth and Emily in 1859.

Blackwell's first lectures were well received. A friend encouraged Blackwell to publish the lectures in book form. Publishing the lectures offered an opportunity to raise money from the sale of the book. It also meant more people could learn about her medical practice and ideas. Blackwell published the lectures as *The Laws of Life in Reference to the Physical Education of Girls* in 1852. Other doctors responded favorably to its release. Blackwell was particularly delighted by the encouraging response from the dean of Geneva Medical College.

A FRIENDLY TALK

As Blackwell struggled uphill in her practice during those first years in New York City, she initially encountered difficulty finding doctors willing to consult on her cases. One day she needed advice concerning an elderly female patient who had pneumonia. She called in a local doctor who had treated her father many years before in Cincinnati. His response after seeing the patient confused Blackwell. He said he had never seen anything like it, adding he did not know what to do. Blackwell was perplexed. The patient clearly had pneumonia —and not even a severe form of it! Blackwell finally realized *she* was the problem. He did not think it appropriate to consult with a female doctor.

Realizing this, Blackwell provided a solution. "I at once assured my old acquaintance that it need not be considered in the light of an ordinary consultation, if he were uneasy about it, but as a friendly talk. So, finally, he gave me his best advice; my patient rapidly got well and happily I never afterwards had any difficulty in obtaining a necessary consultation from members of the profession."[9]

SERVING THE POOR

Despite the uptick in her practice, Blackwell was not happy overall. Her practice did not meet her professional needs. She wanted to help a greater number of people, especially women. She was hungry to learn more. She wanted exposure to different types of illnesses. She yearned for increased professional relationships. Blackwell *still* believed a dispensary was the best way of attaining her goals of increased knowledge and medical relationships. The reality, however, was that none in New York City wanted a woman doctor on staff. She realized only one option existed—to start her own dispensary.

Her friends helped raise money needed to start one. She opened her dispensary in March 1853 in the Thompkins Square area. Later she moved it to Third Street. The dispensary provided free services to poor residents during the three afternoons it was open each week. Its patients sometimes needed more than health services. For this reason, the dispensary sometimes offered other services. It gave out information on finding jobs, recommended charities that could help patients, and sometimes provided short-term small loans.

When it first opened, one of Blackwell's friends assisted with various nonmedical tasks. Over the next two years, the dispensary flourished. It served more people. More of Blackwell's friends supported its work. The dispensary was a success!

CHAPTER FOUR

PARTNERS IN MEDICINE

"... when the novelty of the innovation is past, men and women will be valuable friends in medicine, but for a time that cannot be."[1]
—Elizabeth Blackwell

Elizabeth Blackwell worked day and night to make the dispensary a success. She went where her patients were, never considering their financial situations. She pursued her career and ran the dispensary with compassionate care. Its success prompted Blackwell's incorporation of the facility in 1854.

Blackwell established a name, formal mission statement, operating guidelines (bylaws), and an oversight group (trustees) to whom she would be accountable. The trustees were all men. That was a victory in itself, given how many men still maintained old-fashioned ideas about a woman's place in society, and most male doctors blocked female access to the field.

It was named the New York Dispensary for Poor Women and Children. Blackwell envisioned it as a place where women doctors would treat poor female patients. The purpose and mission for the facility was shared in its First Annual Report. Published on February 8, 1855, it noted:

> The design of this institution is to give to poor women an opportunity of consulting physicians of their own sex. The existing charities of our city regard the employment of women as physicians as an experiment, the success of which has not yet been sufficiently proved to [gain] cordial cooperation. It was therefore necessary to form a separate institution which should furnish to poor women the medical aid which they could not obtain elsewhere.
>
> . . . The Eleventh Ward was chosen as the location for the dispensary, it being destitute of medical charity while possessing a densely crowded poor population. . . . Over 200 women have received medical aid. . . . With all of these patients, the necessity of cleanliness, ventilation, and judicious [sensible] diet has been strongly urged. . . . Poor women may be sent from any part of the city to receive the medical aid of the dispensary, it being free to all.[2]

Monies to start the New York Dispensary for Poor Women and Children were raised by Blackwell's friends. The trustees also started a fundraising campaign to help establish a permanent fund for operating the facility. The goal was $5000. The long-term goals included expanding the dispensary into a full hospital.

Despite the success of the New York Dispensary for Poor Women and Children, worries about money plagued Blackwell. She could not afford to keep renting rooms. She decided to buy a house. She borrowed the money from a friend. She used the house for three purposes, separating the space according to use. She lived in the attic. Her practice was in the basement. She rented the middle rooms to help with expenses.

She encountered other problems. People gossiped about her. Some sent anonymous hate letters. Men made crude remarks while she was out at night visiting patients. She had problems with some police officers. The woman who had beaten all odds by becoming a doctor did not let these things deter her from her goal of providing quality care to her patients. Rather, she believed, ". . . with common sense, self-reliance and attention to the work at hand, any woman can pursue the medical calling without risk."[3]

Blackwell still suffered from lack of camaraderie with male doctors. She wrote to her sister Emily about her concerns. Emily had followed her older

WHAT'S IN A NAME?

There were different terms for doctors during the 1800s. A "woman doctor" often meant someone who performed abortions. Other common terms for doctors were "regular" and "irregular." They were used to describe either the methods doctors used or their education. "Regular" doctors had formal training and degrees from medical schools. They used methods that sometimes were so painful that people got violently ill or died. Some people avoided regular doctors for these reasons. They chose care from "irregular" doctors who used alternative treatments, like the water cure Elizabeth Blackwell had for her infected eye. Other treatments included using herbs, and even hypnosis. When Blackwell's eye was injured, her sister Anna tried hypnosis on her without success. Because women were locked out of the medical field, many became "irregular" doctors. Blackwell wanted to experiment with methods that improved health care without causing additional harm or death. She wanted to train women to do the same as "regular" doctors.

sister's lead and was pursuing a career in medicine. In the May 1854 letter Blackwell told Emily, "One of the most difficult points I have to contend with here is the entire absence of medical sympathy; the medical solitude is really awful at times; I should thankfully turn to any [medically] educated woman if I could find one."[4]

ANOTHER FEMALE DOCTOR IN THE FAMILY

Blackwell was specifically speaking about her time in New York City. Since she graduated from medical college, Blackwell's circle of women in medicine had grown, including Emily. In a May 1850 letter to Emily she mentioned looking forward to her sister joining her in practice.

Emily experienced the same resistance to women in the medical field as her big sister had. She could not even get into Elizabeth's alma mater! Geneva Medical School had closed its doors to women after Elizabeth graduated. Bowing to pressure from the New York Medical Association, the college refused to admit other women. Eventually, Emily was admitted to Rush Medical Center in Chicago. That school locked her out after her first year because of pressure from male doctors in the state.

Western Reserve University welcomed her, however. She graduated with honors in 1854. She left the country seeking postgraduate medical training opportunities abroad. She trained in Scotland,

Emily Blackwell followed in her sister's footsteps, earning a medical degree in 1854. The Blackwell sisters worked together to establish an infirmary for the indigent, with Emily taking on important fundraising responsibilities.

> To her, chiefly, I owed the awakening to the fact that sanitation is the supreme goal of medicine, its foundation, and its crown. . . . When in later years, I entered into practice, extremely skeptical in relation to the value of drugs and ordinary medical methods, my strong faith in hygiene formed the solid ground from which I gradually built up my own methods of treatment.[8]

Blackwell had already set up practice in New York City when Nightingale had her opportunity to make an impact in the nursing field. In 1854, war broke out. Great Britain fought against Russia in the Crimean War. Nurses were needed. Nightingale answered the call. Her heroic, compassionate service made her a hero to wounded men—and in the eyes of people worldwide.

At first, however, Nightingale and the other thirty-eight female nurses were shunned. Doctors preferred using male nurses. Nightingale worked to clean up hospitals she worked in. A growing number of wounded men resulted in an increased need for nursing staff. Eventually, women nurses were allowed to help.

Nightingale worked unceasingly throughout the day. She was known for coming in the wards in the evenings, carrying a lantern and making soldiers as comfortable as possible. Her work did not stop when the war ended. Instead, she devoted her time to training. In 1860, she opened a school for nurses. She was a pioneer

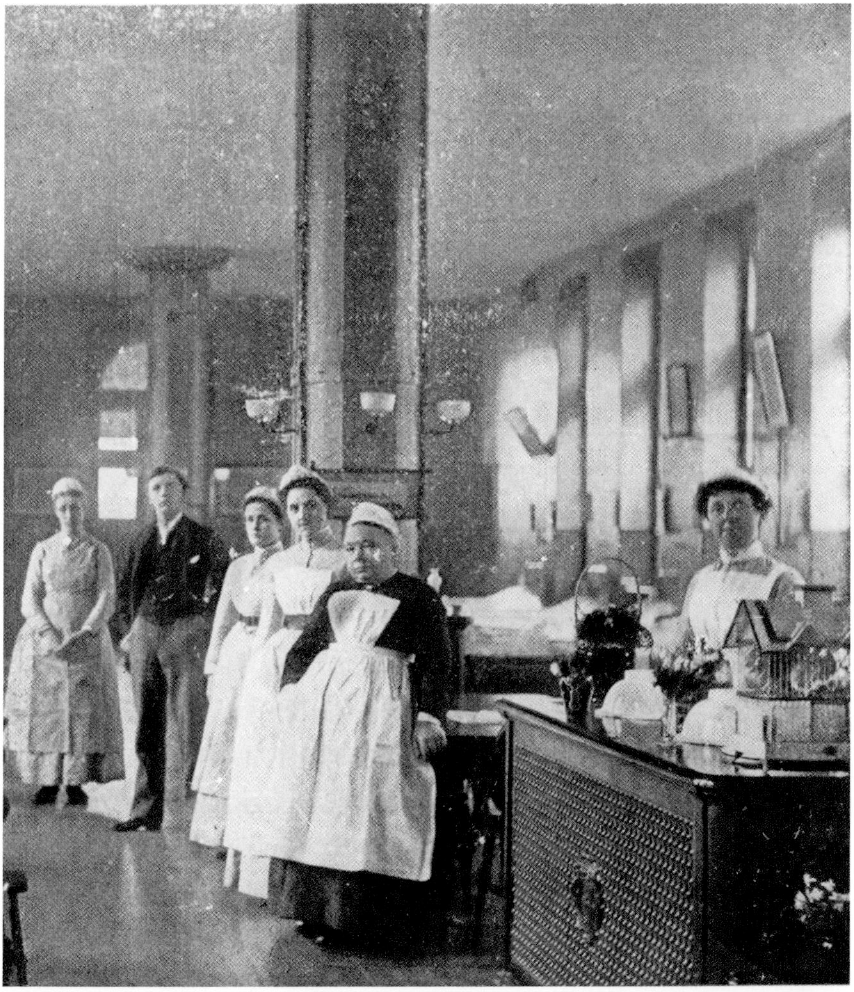

This photo of nurses in a ward at St Thomas's was taken after the establishment of the Nightingale Training School and Home for Nurses in 1860. Thanks to Nightingale, nursing became a popular profession for women.

CHANGING ROLES IN NURSING

Male nurses on a ward often attract attention today. Many people have the impression that it is a new idea for men to enter the nursing field. That is not the case. In fact, when Florence Nightingale dreamed of becoming a nurse, the field was just another area of medicine closed to women. Men worked in hospitals and other facilities and provided professional care to patients under the direction of doctors. Male nurses viewed female nurses in the same way male doctors viewed their female counterparts: they did not want to work with them.

Florence Nightingale's service during the war and in the school she established changed many people's views. She made people realize that women could be caring, helpful professionals even in times of national crises like war. She inspired many women's nursing dreams. The face of nursing has changed since her heroic efforts. In 2011, for example, 91 percent of all nurses were women, according to the US Census Bureau.

in establishing standards for nursing care. Her efforts inspired many women to choose nursing as a career field.

A PROMISING STUDENT

Marie Zakrzewska studied medicine abroad and earned a medical degree in the United States. She joined the Blackwell sisters at the New York Infirmary before founding the New England Hospital for Women and Children.

Marie Zakrzewska had a knack for midwifery. In her early twenties, she enjoyed a successful career. She worked as chief midwife in a hospital in Berlin, Germany. She got the position after the head of the midwifery department recognized her skills and encouraged her to study. When she completed those studies, he appointed her to serve under him as chief. She trained over two hundred students, twenty-five percent of which were men. Her career ended when her supervisor died.

She still wanted to practice midwifery. She came to America because she believed it offered more opportunities than Germany. She tried getting a job in her field, but the German doctors she contacted would not hire her. They suggested she become a nurse. As she desperately searched for help, she was told her to contact Blackwell. She came to see Blackwell in May 1854. Blackwell was able to speak German with Zakrzewska, who spoke no English.

Blackwell was immediately impressed by Zakrzewska's skills. Writing about her to Emily she said, "I have found a student in whom I can take a great deal of interest. . . . There is true stuff in her, and I shall do my best to bring it out. She must obtain a medical degree."[9]

Zakrzewska first needed to learn English, find a suitable college, and obtain funding to go to school. Blackwell helped her with each of these. She tutored Zakrzewska in English. She guided her October 1854 enrollment at Western Reserve University, Emily Blackwell's alma mater. She got others to pay for Zakrzewska's college costs. The two women maintained their friendship and professional connections. After she graduated from Cleveland Medical College, Zakrzewska joined the staff of Blackwell's New York City dispensary.

A CONSTANT COMPANION

In the height of her loneliness in 1854, Blackwell adopted Katharine Barry. Barry was a seven-year-old orphan. She lived at an orphanage on Randall's Island. Many children living at the orphanage were German and Russian immigrants. Others were Irish like Barry, whom Blackwell nicknamed Kitty.

The two became inseparable over the years. Kitty was a faithful friend and constant companion. She never married, instead choosing to live with Blackwell and help out in a secretarial capacity when older. A birthday present from Kitty two years after being adopted by Blackwell prompted Blackwell to write, “On this bright Sunday morning I feel full of hope and strength for the future. . . . Who will ever guess the restorative support which that poor little orphan has been to me? When I took her to live with me . . . [it] was a dark time and she did me good.”[10]

CHAPTER FIVE

WAR ON SICKNESS AND DISEASE

> "I understand now why this life has never been lived before. It *is* hard, with no support but a high purpose, to live against every species of social opposition . . ."[1]
> —Elizabeth Blackwell

With both Emily and Marie Zakrzewska in New York City in 1856, Blackwell felt she was given an invaluable gift—the opportunity to open the hospital of her dreams. Plans involved expanding the existing dispensary into an infirmary.

Emily, Elizabeth, and "Dr. Zak"—as she was called—started fundraising. They found an ideal property for the hospital, a house for rent at 64 Bleecker Street. It was in the Greenwich Village section, a poor area lacking hospitals and doctors. Poor residents had no money to travel farther, for health care needed a facility like the one the three doctors planned.

On May 12, 1857, the hospital opened its doors. The New York Infirmary for Women and Children

Along with her sister Emily and Marie Zakrzewska, Elizabeth Blackwell opened the New York Infirmary for Women and Children. The facility was run by women to treat women.

was ready to receive patients! Elizabeth was the director. Dr. Zak was the resident physician. Emily headed up surgery. It was a unique facility run by women for women. Nothing like it existed. Its uniqueness prompted many objections. People gave them many reasons why the hospital could not succeed. Some of those reasons were noted in the hospital's 1864 Annual Report. They included:

> . . . female doctors would be looked upon with so much suspicion that the police would interfere; . . . if deaths occurred their death certificates would not be recognized; . . . without men as resident physicians they would not be able to control the patients; . . . and, finally, that they would never be able to collect enough money for so unpopular an effort.[2]

The doctors did not let needing money stop them. The women doctors thought of creative ways to raise funds. They gave lectures. They sponsored concerts. They held a bazaar for seven consecutive years. People as far away as England donated items for sale.

The infirmary exceeded expectations. It treated hundreds of patients in its first few months. High demand continued. The doctors added interns to the staff to help with the workload. It did not encounter as many troubles as predicted. However, one incident stands out.

A patient died while having her baby. Her angry relatives protested outside. They carried weapons—shovels and pickaxes. They accused the lady doctors of using cold water, which killed their loved one. They were wrong; the doctors had not used the alternative "cure" used by irregular doctors. The victim's family wanted to get into the hospital. Whether they would have hurt the doctors is unknown. Police officers showed up just in time. They stopped the protest. They reasoned with the family. They explained that no doctor can save *every* patient. The family could not argue with that truth. They left. The doctors were safe—again.

FIGHTING AGAINST CONTAGIOUS DISEASES

Contagious diseases spread quickly due to the way people disposed of waste products. Plumbing and sewage systems were not as advanced as they are today. Waste would end up in the water. People used the water for drinking and cooking. Poisons from the waste products made them ill. Blackwell became an advocate for clean drinking water. She spoke about the need for water to be safe for personal use and cooking. People did not always have clean water for washing their bodies. Bacteria and other agents easily attached to their bodies, making them sick—or sicker. Blackwell tried to change this. She especially shared the need for women to clean their bodies properly.

Blackwell knew from her work with Florence Nightingale that her patients would never enjoy good health for long periods of time if they did not change their habits. She instructed them on particular areas to improve. Society was not used to such plain speech. Such topics were once considered taboo for public discussion. Blackwell, however, believed that was part of the problem. She believed girls and women needed to know how to properly care for their bodies, washing them to remove dirt, odors, and any bacteria.

Today, it is a common practice for doctors to wash their hands and put on gloves before examining a patient. It was not so when Blackwell practiced medicine. She believed a key to good patient care and disease prevention was hand washing. From her work with Florence Nightingale, she knew that dirty hands posed tremendous health risks. Today doctors know; putting dirty hands in the mouth or eyes, for example, could cause or spread disease.

Blackwell also told doctors the same thing. She warned that not cleaning one's hands after a visit with a patient potentially could spread the first person's illness to the next person . . . and the next . . . and next. Doctors began listening to her. They started using more sanitary methods

OTHER BATTLES

In Blackwell's time, people did not realize the cause of some sicknesses. They did not realize that dirty water, filthy hands, and improper disposal of waste (human and animal) could make them sick. Blackwell helped them understand how all of those played a part in health. She encouraged women to take more active roles in keeping their families healthy.

While Blackwell waged her war on sickness and disease, two other battles raged in America and in England. First, slavery prevailed. It was hotly contested in both countries by abolitionists who felt that the inhuman treatments of blacks needed to stop. Women joined the effort. They formed women antislavery societies because men blocked them from serving in those headed by men. One of the first was organized by abolitionist Lucretia Mott. Working to end slavery

Lucretia Mott was a leading women's rights advocate. While the suffragette movement raged, Blackwell focused on advocating for women's health.

opened women's eyes to their own situations. They realized they, too, had little voice or influence in society.

Second, the women were fighting for new rights. Women in both countries had long been denied political and social status whereby they could significantly contribute to society. Women were treated as if they were second-class citizens. Their opinions did not matter. They were expected to take care of their homes and families. New manufacturing processes spurred the beginning of the industrial revolution. More workers were needed. Factories offered jobs. They employed men, women, and children in horrendous conditions.

Women protested the working conditions of women and children. They protested the low salaries of women who earned less than men. They shared concerns about the long hours children and women worked. Eventually they petitioned for the right to vote. They knew that if they could vote they could influence different laws.

In 1848, the first Women's Rights Convention had been held in Seneca Falls, New York. Blackwell had friends who actively led the women's rights movement. She read the materials from the convention, but did not join the cause. She believed the issues raised by suffragists were important. But she did not believe she was called to be an active participant. Her fight was against sickness and disease, and against bad moral behavior. ". . . I must keep my energy for what seems to me a deeper movement," she wrote in a letter to her family.[3]

Even her family's involvement in the movement did not change her mind. Her brother's wife, Lucy Stone, started the American Women's Suffrage Association in 1869. She was the coeditor of the *Woman's Journal* in 1870. Two years later, Stone ran it with her husband, Henry Blackwell. Years later, their daughter, Alice Stone Blackwell, also became a well-known figure in the women's rights movement. But not Elizabeth Blackwell. As they fought these issues, Blackwell focused on sickness and disease.

She took her fight abroad. For a year, from August 1858 to August 1859, Elizabeth Blackwell visited England. She lived there with Kitty. She went to help advance opportunities for women in medicine, and to get listed on a special registry of United Kingdom doctors.

In England there were no female doctors. Hospitals catering only to women also did not exist. Blackwell's guidance could help change that. Many people had heard of her success in the United States. They wanted more information. People had asked her on occasion to come share about their experiences and why the work was needed. Blackwell traveled to England to share information about the strides American women were making in medicine. She promoted medical education for women by giving lectures, and speaking with prominent individuals. She spoke about the importance of knowing how the body works, and of having formal medical training. She also talked about the practical work female doctors did in America.

Blackwell prepared a series of lectures. She delivered her first lecture on March 2, 1859. The tremendous positive response prompted a call to develop a women's hospital in England. A circular, or business flier, promoted the hospital's creation and requested donations. It was signed by numerous influential women, titled the "Proposed Hospital for Treatment of the Special Diseases of Women." It noted:

> The lectures recently delivered by Doctor Elizabeth Blackwell . . . have produced in the minds of the ladies who heard them a strong conviction of the necessity for a more general diffusion of hygienic knowledge among women; and have led to a proposition to found a hospital for a class of diseases, the ordinary treatment of which too frequently involves much avoidable moral suffering, to be placed under the direction of competent women physicians, in connection with a Board of consulting physicians and surgeons.[4]

Blackwell provided guidance on the proposed hospital during the rest of her stay in England.

Blackwell's other reason for going to England involved an official list—or medical registry—being developed of all doctors permitted to practice throughout the United Kingdom. To make the list, she needed to be practicing in the country before the cut-off date of October 1, 1858. Blackwell made the deadline. She became the first woman listed on the registry. After completing her purposes abroad, Blackwell returned to the America in August 1859.

FAREWELL DR. ZAK

In 1859, Dr. Zak left the infirmary. She moved to Boston to take a job at the New England Medical College in Boston. She met resistance from its founders, trustees, and students when she tried to improve the training. The college's founder had been trained as an "irregular" doctor and saw no need for much of the training Dr. Zak proposed.

Because of their differing opinions about doctor training, she did not get approval to bring in new instruments for teaching students how to use them in everyday medical situations. She felt the students were not receiving a proper education or training. She faced problem after problem. She left the school in 1861. She started a hospital, calling it the New England Hospital for Women and Children.

BATTLING THE CIVIL WAR

The New York Infirmary for Women and Children thrived. Patients kept coming. In 1861, the infirmary moved to a larger facility to meet the increased demand. Blackwell was ready to start another dream idea: a medical college. She wanted to train women as doctors and nurses. She wanted them properly trained so they could enter the medical field with excellent credentials. In 1861, while they were planning, the Civil War broke out. It changed everything. The plan to open the women's college was shelved.

The Civil War was a battle between Southern and Northern states. Slavery was a dividing issue. The South wanted to protect its right to keep slaves. The North wanted to abolish slavery. Blackwell wrote, "As the deadly contest proceeded, and every town and village sent forth its volunteers . . . the concentration of thought and action on the war dwarfed every other effort . . . we threw ourselves energetically into the cause of freedom."[5]

From an early age, Blackwell was raised with the belief that slavery was wrong. As an adult, she had witnessed it in Kentucky, North Carolina, and South Carolina. She hated how slavery dehumanized slaves. She believed strongly in what her upbringing had taught her, that all were created equal. She wanted to help. She was willing to put her practice on hold to help support the Union's efforts.

Blackwell knew the need for civilian help would be great. She helped organize a meeting at the infirmary for other women interested in helping. About fifty women attended. The group wanted to collect money and practical items. Warm socks, canned goods, and blankets topped the list. Other supplies were added, including paper for writing letters home. It became clear that an organization was needed to help lead the efforts. The Women's Central Relief Association (WCRA) was formed. More showed up to its first meeting than expected thanks to a notice in the *New York Times*, a prominent newspaper that still exists today.

The WRCA held "Sanitary Fairs" as its primary fundraiser. People paid money to attend. They viewed the various exhibits on display, and could buy items when they were auctioned off at the event. The fairs raised thousands of dollars. The WRCA later became the US Sanitary Aid Commission, a volunteer organization approved by the war department.

Thanks to the efforts of Dorothea Dix, the mentally ill had a safe place to be treated.

CHAMPION FOR MENTALLY ILL PERSONS

Dorothea Dix was born in 1802 in Hampton, Maine. She moved to Boston when she was twelve to live with her rich grandmother because her parents could not take care of their three children. Dix was a teacher for years before quitting due to tuberculosis, a lung disease. As she was getting better, she visited a Massachusetts jail. She was shocked. Patients with mental illnesses were there with criminals! It became her life's work to advocate for changes in treatment for the mentally ill.

She began speaking out against the treatment. She gathered information revealing patient care. It shocked people. Few knew the horrific conditions mentally ill individuals endured. Dix stressed the importance of treating people with dignity and respect. She called for equal treatment, noting that mentally ill people should be given the same quality of care as other people with *any* sickness. They should not be jailed simply because they had a mental illness. She advocated in America and in Europe. Her efforts helped get laws changed. She was asked to lead the US Sanitary Aid Commission because of the great work she did. She died in 1887.

Dorothea Dix was selected to serve as the Commission's superintendent.

Elizabeth Blackwell was an important organizer of the nursing volunteers. She handpicked women she believed were ready to handle emergency situations. She especially looked for those who had some medical knowledge, or who could easily learn about wound care, hygiene, sanitation, and other important care issues. "All that could be done in the extreme urgency of the need," Blackwell wrote, "was sift out the most promising women from the multitudes that applied to be sent on as nurses, put them for a month in training at the great Bellevue Hospital of New York . . . and send the[m] on for distribution to Miss. Dix."[6] Following in Florence Nightingale's steps, these women provided invaluable service. Meanwhile, Dr. Zak was also working in Boston to train nurses.

The Civil War lasted four years. Close to three million men fought in the war. About 620,000 men died during the war. Of that number, it is estimated that about two-thirds died from disease, not from injuries. That equals more than 410,000 men! Many different diseases plagued soldiers. Factors causing disease included many of the things Elizabeth Blackwell had long fought against—poor hygiene, dirty drinking water, and poor sanitation. Diseases spread easily because soldiers lived in overcrowded, dirty areas with limited access to clean water and nutritious food. They did not have

The high number of casualties in the Civil War brought about the need for—and acceptance of—female nurses.

methods of protecting against bugs, lice, flies, and other pests. In addition, the soldiers were exposed to extreme weather.

The staggering numbers of sick and wounded soldiers fueled the urgent need for trained nurses. At first female nurses were shunned. They experienced the same discrimination as female doctors. Men did not want to work with them. Many soldiers did not want to be treated by females. But as the number of wounded and sick rose, women encountered less resistance. Their efforts were needed—and appreciated.

CHAPTER SIX

MEDICAL REVOLUTIONARY

"In 1869 the early pioneer work in America was ended."[1]
—Elizabeth Blackwell

As the end of the war drew near, Elizabeth Blackwell received an invitation from the Nursing Corps to visit its headquarters in Washington, DC. She accepted. One of the highlights of the June 1864 trip was meeting President Abraham Lincoln. She never had the opportunity again. Less than nine months later, he was killed.

Abraham Lincoln was president during the US Civil War, an event that increased the need for medical professionals.

The end of the Civil War marked changes in the United States. Soldiers returning from war needed medical care. Many suffered

ABRAHAM LINCOLN

Abraham Lincoln was born on February 12, 1809, in Hardin County, Kentucky. He had several different jobs before becoming a lawyer and a politician. He ran for president and won, becoming the sixteenth president of the United States. States in the south were angry. They knew Lincoln opposed slavery. They worried that they would have to give up their slaves. Seven states decided to leave the Union. They left before his inauguration in March 1861.

President Lincoln took office nonetheless. He refused to allow the country to split. He believed the Constitution did not allow it. The Civil War broke out in 1861 partly because of the conflict. Two years into the war, in 1863, President Lincoln issued the Emancipation Proclamation. It ordered slaves in some states to be freed.

President Abraham was reelected in 1864. On April 9, 1865, the Confederate Army surrendered to the Union Army. That date is considered the end of the Civil War.

People were angry. John Wilkes Booth was one. He shot President Lincoln on April 14, 1865. It happened at Ford's Theater in Washington, DC. President Lincoln died the next day. His death shocked the world.

life-changing wounds. Soldiers' families needed money and other resources. Similarly, former slaves faced many challenges adjusting to their new lives.

Slaves had choices to make, whether to stay in the areas where they had been in bondage or to move on. They needed plenty of help, especially as many could not read or write. They had no money. Housing, clothing, jobs, and other resources were provided partly by organizations that had previously been heavily involved in fighting slavery. Like the soldiers returning from war, the former slaves also needed medical care.

Interest in the medical field was high among women who had served as wartime nurses. They had enjoyed historic freedom working for a common cause and saw the fruit of their labors. Many wanted to become nurses, others doctors. Yet, with the end of the war, they still faced many roadblocks. They also still could not vote.

Following the Civil War, leading women physicians continued to pursue a dual strategy. They maintained and strengthened their separate women's medical sphere, all the while advocating their ultimate goal—expanded opportunities for women in the male medical establishment.[2] By this time, women were being trained at women's colleges in Boston, and Philadelphia, but Blackwell believed they were not being held to sufficiently high standards and thus were not able to do the job later, proving arguments against them. To combat this, she encouraged the

Nursing schools became more popular after the Civil War, and many young women trained for this profession. Many who had served as war nurses went on to become physicians, thanks to Blackwell's medical school.

trustees of the infirmary to apply for a college charter, which was granted in 1865.[3]

Despite some reservations, the Blackwell doctors started planning the college, but it was put on hold before the war began. Elizabeth Blackwell explained, "We took this step, however, with hesitation for our own feeling was adverse to the formation of an entirely separate school for women."[4] The trustees started a college fund to raise monies.

While the college was being planned, Blackwell ramped up the infirmary's mission to help promote healthy family lifestyles through health and nutrition. She created a job called "sanitary worker" in 1866.

> [W]e established [the position of] sanitary visitor . . . filled by one of our assistant physicians, whose special duty it was to give simple, practical instruction to poor mothers on the management of infants and the preservation of the health of their families. An intelligent young coloured [black] physician, Dr. Cole, who was one of our resident assistants, carried on this work with tact and care. Experience of its results serve to show that the establishment of such a department would be a valuable addition to every hospital.[5]

Cole was the . . . first black graduate of the Woman's Medical College of Philadelphia and the second regularly trained black woman physician in the United States.[6] Blackwell felt doctors should be involved in giving parents as much information as possible to help them have healthy families. "It has always seemed to me . . . that the first and constant aim of the family physician should be to diffuse the sanitary knowledge which would enable parents to bring up healthy children."[7]

A BETTER SCHOOL STRUCTURE

In developing the college, Blackwell wanted to design the best courses and training possible. For example, the college's required classes included hygiene. It was equally as important as other classes. Other schools did not consider it such a big deal. Elizabeth Blackwell was the professor of hygiene. The sanitary worker also reported to her. She believed every hospital should have a sanitary worker on staff. Her goal was to provide excellent medical school training for that person.

Blackwell wanted graduates of her medical school to have superior skills. She wanted them to be able to pass the toughest tests based on acquired knowledge and skills. She did not want the school's professors involved in testing to prevent doctors from saying the students somehow received favorable test results from their teachers. She, therefore, created an independent "examination board." It was made up of well-known, highly respected doctors who did *not* work for the college. This board would be responsible for giving students their final exams. Because of the reputation of each board member, there would be no doubt that students graduating from Blackwell's school were qualified to become doctors.

One other change she made involved the amount of time students' attended medical school. She expanded it by one year. The overall goal was to make the college one of the best medical schools existing at the time. After much planning, the college was ready. On November 2, 1868, the Women's Medical College of New York opened. A lecture room at New

This illustration from *Frank Leslie's Illustrated Newspaper* depicts students attending an anatomy lecture at Elizabeth Blackwell's Women's Medical College of New York.

York University served as a temporary location. The college planned on renting the house next to the infirmary when it became available. They also planned on buying a property in the future.

A SUCCESS!

The Women's Medical College of the New York Infirmary was a success. As designed, the college was revolutionary for its time. It mirrored Elizabeth Blackwell's pioneering spirit. Across the country, women were gaining further ground in the medical field. Throughout the [n]orthern states, the free and equal entrance of women into the profession of medicine [had been] secured. In Boston, New York, and Philadelphia special medical schools for women were designated . . . and in some long-established colleges women were received as students in ordinary classes.[8] Blackwell is credited with opening doors for these women.

The race to be first is a worldwide effort that mainly focuses on achievement. It often overlooks the challenges, struggles, and personal sacrifices needed to be a pioneer. Sometimes the person who actually wins the honor of being first is someone who came to the race as a reluctant participant and ends up a shining star. Elizabeth Blackwell was such a star.

The very first female doctor in the United States, she ran her race without a map or course to follow.

She often ran alone, with few people cheering her on. Her list of accomplishments is impressive. She was by all accounts a pioneer, a medical revolutionary who very few people expected to see at the top of her field.

A LADY DOCTOR

The primary challenge Blackwell faced was being a female. In her day, "woman doctor" was a term used for doctors who performed abortions. Men were skeptical of her, thinking she only wanted to focus on that part of doctoring. As she became more well known and respected, people started calling her a "lady doctor." It was a way of distancing her from the term that was not flattering to women in medicine. Over time, the term "woman doctor" broadened to simply mean female doctors.

Blackwell's family raised her to be ladylike. At the same time, they taught her to be passionate about social justice and to speak up for the oppressed. Blackwell never forgot her early training. She did not barge into the medical field demanding special treatment or favors. She did not try to earn a special place in college by pretending to be weak and fearful. That was not how she was raised! She refused to pretend to be something she was not.

When friends suggested she put on men's clothing and go to Paris to medical school, she refused. She wanted to learn her craft on American

Elizabeth Blackwell's life is a lesson in tenacity. She refused to be denied the opportunity to practice medicine. After breaking down so many barriers, she created opportunities for subsequent generations of women doctors.

soil as the lady she was raised to be. She exhibited the grit her family instilled in her. Through persistence she landed her spot at Geneva Medical College. By not giving up she helped other women stick to their dreams, too.

Before Blackwell entered the medical field, women were often too ashamed to mention their very personal health care concerns to male doctors. Doctors also did not perform certain examinations. Male doctors also could never understand issues related to the female body's operation that might not be covered in their textbook. Blackwell had a distinct advantage. She was a woman. She knew how female bodies work. Blackwell used her first-hand knowledge of female bodies paired with her technical training to help girls and women understand how to care for theirs. In doing so, she was a pioneer in women's health, especially in gynecology, labor, and delivery.

She did not shy away from sensitive topics. At all times, she was a lady, but she was also Samuel Blackwell's daughter. She would fight to help those she believed needed her most. She would offer a unique perspective that men could not offer female patients. She would be adamant about providing them with the best quality service already afforded to male patients. Her insightful lectures captured listeners' hearts while elevating their knowledge of medical issues.

DILIGENCE PAYS OFF

Blackwell had no misconceptions about the field she was about to enter. She knew it was dominated by men. She knew those men did not want a female joining their ranks. She knew that many would not help her reach her goals. Each of these factors can be a barrier that keeps any person from trying something new. Together, they would have provided enough fuel for Blackwell to run away—not toward—her dreams. Yet, Blackwell pursued her career field with diligence.

She diligently studied. She put her heart into her various internships. She graduated top of her class. She traveled to England for training denied her in America. She proved a woman could succeed in a male-dominated world—in any country! Her diligence provided an example for other women to follow.

A LEADER ARISES

Blackwell did not enter medicine with an agenda to be a leader in the field. She solely wanted to achieve a goal she felt was her life's purpose. It did not take long for Blackwell to emerge as a leader. Once she earned the title in the United States, she took deliberate steps to open doors closed to women in England.

When the Women's Medical College of New York opened in 1869, its success was quick. It met a need.

Women were waiting for such a school just for them. One of the students in the first class was Sophia Jex-Blake. She was visiting from England and later would return there. Eventually, she would become a member of the staff of a hospital Blackwell helped organize in England as well.

With the opening of the medical college, she made a way for women to receive rigorous training, rivaling other schools. If students doubted their career goal and whether being a doctor was possible, they only had to look at the college's female medical staff. Those doctors were proof that women could succeed in the medical field, if they put in the hard work necessary. Blackwell was satisfied with how everything turned out. It had been a hard road to get to this point. Much had been accomplished in America since she graduated medical school.

She was ready to take up a new challenge. Blackwell planned her return to England, believing her work was done in America. She had laid a strong foundation for women to stand upon in the medical field. She was ready to return to her birthplace. She wrote, "Our New York centre [sic] was well organized under able guidance, and I determined to return to England for a temporary though prolonged residence, both to renew physical strength . . . as well as to assist in the pioneer work so bravely commencing [there]."[9]

CHAPTER SEVEN

LATER YEARS

"The more I see of work in England, the more I like it."[1]
—Elizabeth Blackwell

In 1869, Elizabeth Blackwell sailed to England with Kitty. Blackwell wanted to make a greater impact on the medical field there. She set up offices, lectured on topics of hygiene, the need for female doctors, and more. At the Working Women's College in England she spoke on "How to Keep a Household in Health." This lecture laid down rules of health for the guidance of poor women in the management of their households and was welcomed by the audience."[2]

FIGHTING AGAINST UNFAIR LAWS

One of the meetings she attended soon after touring London added a new focus to her work. In 1869, she attended the Social Sciences Congress. There she learned about a movement to repeal—or end—the "Contagious Diseases Acts." The laws were established to curb sexually transmitted diseases, but they ended up promoting prostitution. Learning more about the laws jarred Blackwell's memory of her days at St. Bartholomew's. She worked in a ward where women were placed because of the diseases they contracted.

Blackwell hated the idea of women working as prostitutes and in other sexually related jobs. She felt those jobs encouraged sin and abuse of women. Beginning in 1869, Blackwell became a tough opponent against the Contagious Disease Acts. For seventeen years, she fought with others to have them repealed. In 1886, their efforts paid off. The Contagious Disease Acts were repealed.

The Princess's visit to the London School of Medicine for Women on Monday, to open the new Science Laboratories had been eagerly anticipated, and the students gave a hearty welcome to the Royal party. The Prince accompanied his wife, and there was the usual presentation of bouquets and purses, the Princess afterwards going over the building with Mrs. Garrett Anderson. In her address of welcome, Mrs. Anderson called attention to the fact that the London School of Medicine for Women had been open for twenty-four years— the number of students now amounting to 170. The Pfeiffer block which the Princess opened had cost some 9,000*l*. or 10,000*l*. Additional funds for completing the whole block of buildings are still urgently needed. The Prince of Wales, in his speech replying to the address of thanks to the Princess, stated that he had himself last week made a tour of the laboratories, and had been much interested to find the women students working so assiduously. The Princess and himself were much gratified to learn of the good work accomplished by qualified medical women at home and in India, where their presence in the zenanas was most valuable.

A Corner of the New Science Laboratories
THE LONDON SCHOOL OF MEDICINE FOR WOMEN

Inside the New Science Laboratories
THE LONDON SCHOOL OF MEDICINE FOR WOMEN

Blackwell cofounded the London School of Medicine for Women after moving to England in 1869.

Blackwell continued to be called on to support other health projects. In 1871, she met with people desiring to provide public education on sanitary issues. One outcome of the meeting was the National Health Society. The group's purpose was summed up in its motto, "Prevention is better than cure."

LONDON SCHOOL OF MEDICINE FOR WOMEN

Blackwell cofounded the London School of Medicine for Women in 1874 with Elizabeth Garrett Anderson and Sophia Jex-Blake. Blackwell considered Garrett Anderson "the pioneer of the medical movement in England."[3] They met in 1859 when Blackwell was lecturing in England. One person wrote a letter to a local paper attacking the lecture.

Others sent in anonymous requests for her to answer their personal problems on the subject. True to her commitment to never give out medical advice by letter, she did not respond to any of these. She wrote, ". . . I was overwhelmed by . . . letters from persons in all classes of society, requesting medical advice on the most important and delicate subjects—subjects which are only suitable for confidential counsel of the physician's consulting-room, where alone advice adapted to each individual case can be judiciously given."[4]

Garrett was unmarried at the time. Her interest in medicine began as she listened to Blackwell.

Blackwell established the London School of Medicine for Women with Sophia Jex-Blake and Elizabeth Garrett Anderson (above). Like Blackwell, Elizabeth Garrett Anderson was something of a pioneer, becoming the first woman in England to qualify as a physician.

While finishing up at the University of London, she searched without success to enter medical school. In a couple instances, her admittance was rejected by a very small margin. It was frustrating to learn she was so close to being admitted.

In a May 8, 1862, letter, she shared her struggles with Blackwell. She added, ". . . I am more than ever convinced both that this special work is one which a woman may have a divine right to engage in, and that every single woman's life is both happier and more useful if she has an absorbing interest and pursuit."[5]

Garrett applied and was accepted into the Society of Apothecaries. It allowed her to quickly enter the medical field. She was then listed on the Medical Registry of all doctors approved to practice in Great Britain. She opened two medical facilities. The St. Mary's Dispensary for Women opened in 1866. She started the New Hospital for Women in 1872. The London School of Medicine for Women grew out of that hospital.

Jex-Blake was a former student at the Women's Medical College of New York. She later encountered problems while attending Edinburgh University in Scotland. She was labeled a trouble-maker for her actions involving protests. Her failing grades prompted her to accuse her professors of sexism, which also hurt her reputation. Blackwell and Garrett allowed Jex-Blake to work with them, despite her past antics. At the London School of

Medicine for Women, Blackwell was the professor of gynecology. She taught hygiene and lectured on midwifery. Blackwell wrote, "The work of Dr. Garrett Anderson and Dr. Sophia Jex Blake will always be remembered. It was my privilege and pleasure in some small degree to encourage these brave workers in their pioneer enterprise in England."[6]

She also continued writing, and at times gave other lectures outside of the college. Blackwell had long opposed using animals in experiments. She wrote about the topic, explaining why she felt so passionately that the practice should not be used.

TACKLING TOUGH TOPICS

In 1879, she wrote a new book about sexual education. It was titled *Counsel to Parents on the Moral Education of their Children*. It was a frank book on a topic people did not want shared in public. The book touched on many areas of sex education openly discussed today. In 1879, many people felt the topic was off-limits. Blackwell's friend warned her about publishing it. She predicted Blackwell's reputation would be ruined. She warned, Blackwell's "name would be a forbidden word in England."[7]

Blackwell believed in her book. She felt it was needed. She did not fear being shunned or ignored by society. She could not get a publisher to print it. About a dozen said no. She printed a small edition herself. She finally found one publisher that was willing to publish her book. There was a catch, however. A group of clergy first needed to review it. They agreed Blackwell's book should be published. However, they felt Blackwell should revise the title to reflect the fact that the book contained medical information. They believed this adjustment would generate a more positive public response to Blackwell's work. Thus, *Counsel to Parents on the Moral Education of their Children* became *The Moral Education of the Young, considered under Medical and Social Aspects.*

The clergy were right. People in England and the United States applauded its release. Blackwell wrote about the publication of the book in her autobiography because she wanted to encourage others to continue speaking and writing about moral topics. Since she was able to get her book published, she believed that they, too, would find audiences for their moral work.

RETIREMENT TIME

In 1879, She moved to Rock House in Hastings, England, with Kitty. Although Blackwell initially said she was moving to England temporarily, she ended up living at Rock House for thirty years. She never lived in America again. Blackwell wrote other books. They were *Christian Socialism*, *Wrong and Right Methods of Dealing with the Social Evil*, and *The*

Human Element of Sex. Her traveling included lectures in Paris in 1889.

Blackwell health was failing. She could not work as a doctor. She retired in 1894. In 1895, Blackwell published her autobiography. *Pioneer Women In Opening the Medical Profession to Women* was well received.

NEW YORK PROGRESS

Meanwhile in New York, Blackwell's influence on women's presence in the medical field continued. In 1899, the New York Women's Medical College closed. It had outlived its purposes. There was no longer a need for a school just for women. Medical schools were regularly admitting female students. Blackwell always believed in the benefits of co-ed medical colleges. Since few early medical schools wanted to admit women, she started a women's college. She hoped, however, that one day women's colleges would not be needed simply because females were blocked from medical schools. Students who wanted to transferred to Cornell University Medical School.

A PIONEER DIES

Blackwell made her final trip to the United States in 1906. She was eighty-five years old. She enjoyed seeing a large extended family. Many of those

Elizabeth Blackwell died in 1910 at the age of eighty-nine after suffering a stroke. Her ashes were bere buried at St Munn's Parish Church, Kilmun, Scotland.

attending had heard about the legendary doctor, but had not met her—or seen her in years.

She returned to England and became ill. Before dying she would receive good news. Dr. Blackwell learned that William Smith of Geneva gave Hobart College, the former Geneva Medical College, almost $500,000 to endow a school for women—William Smith College. The college used Smith's donation to erect a hall of science in which biological and psychological laboratories were established.[8]

Elizabeth Blackwell died on May 31, 1910. Kitty was with her. She was buried in Scotland, according to her wishes. Public reaction to her death was swift. Around the world people celebrated her for achieving the distinction of becoming the first woman to be a doctor and for making such tremendous strides for women.

LASTING LEGACY

Elizabeth Blackwell's dream of becoming a doctor became a lifelong pursuit. She became a champion of the poor, providing high-quality health care for free. She stressed the importance of acquiring excellent skills, and helping other women achieve those. Throughout her professional life, she emphasized the importance of good sanitation and personal hygiene in maintaining good health.[9]

Over time, she was recognized as a pioneer. During and after her life she was honored for her work. Numerous honors have been made in her memory. Many books have been written about her inspirational life. A dormitory at William Smith College for Women was named for her in 1906. The school also instituted an award bearing her name.

In 1974, a US postal stamp bearing her image was released. The stamp was a symbol of the recognition of Blackwell's influence.

Women have been able to achieve so much in the medical field because of Blackwell's pioneering example. Other honors include a portrait of Blackwell in the London School of Medicine.

Her alma mater has created a scholarship in Blackwell's name. Hobart & William Smith Colleges offers the Elizabeth Blackwell Class of 1849 Pioneer in Science Scholarship. This prestigious scholarship provides a $25,000 award to first-year students.

More recently, Radcliffe Institute for Advanced Study at Harvard University's Schlesinger Library received a grant to digitize her papers. The extensive online archive includes letters, diaries, and other important documents regarding Blackwell and her family. The library also released an exhibition called the "Women of the Blackwell Family."

NOTABLE ACHIEVEMENTS

Notable achievements of other female doctors were made possible by the very first steps Elizabeth Blackwell took to become a doctor. Some notable achievements include the following. In 1864, Rebecca Lee Crumpler was the first black woman to earn a medical degree when she graduated from the New England Female Medical College.

In 1947, Dr. Gerty Cori became the first woman to receive the Nobel Prize in Medicine. She died in 1957. In 1990, Dr. Antonia Novello became the top doctor in America when she was appointed as US Surgeon General. She was also the first Hispanic to serve in the job. Her term ended in 1996. In 1998, the American Medical Association elected its first female president, Dr. Nancy Dickey.

When Blackwell opened her offices, infirmary, and college, she settled in the slums of New York City. She wanted to be where the need was greatest. The hospital she founded later became known as the New York Downtown Hospital. On September 11, 2001, the hospital she founded was in the ideal place to be of greatest service

In the 1970s, Elizabeth Blackwell's pioneering achievements were celebrated on a US postal stamp. Blackwell's commitment to health and hygiene and her unwavering dedication to her calling have inspired women for generations.

when terrorists attacked the Twin Towers. In the years since, the hospital faced increasing financial troubles, and in 2013, the hospital cut its doctor training program. New York Presbyterian Hospital has since taken over management.

CHOICES, CHOICES

What do you want to be when you grow up? Students either hate or love the question. Among those who hate it, are boys and girls who have not yet decided on a life's goal. Being asked about it time and time again becomes annoying!

Those who love the question usually have an idea of what they want to be—or they have several ideas. They like to talk about the possibilities. It is fun to dream about the many choices available—even if that changes each day! Actually, it is okay to change your mind. Many adults are in careers they never thought about doing. That is especially true for women, including Elizabeth Blackwell, who had no early dreams of becoming a doctor.

Once the idea took root, however, she pursued medicine completely. She sought a career. She found a lifelong devotion to medicine. Throughout her professional life, she emphasized the importance of good sanitation and personal hygiene in maintaining good health. More than a century after her death, Elizabeth Blackwell is remembered as a doctor who transformed women's health care.

Walk into most medical facilities today, and women doctors are among the staff caring for patients. They have earned degrees in various fields of medicine. They use advanced equipment and technological tools that Blackwell could never have imagined when she began her search for "an absorbing career." They are able to enjoy absorbing careers in large part because of Elizabeth Blackwell, the first woman doctor.

In discussing her book on *The Moral Education of the Young, considered under Medical and Social Aspects,* Blackwell wrote, "It has become clear to me that our medical profession has not yet fully realized the special and weighty responsibility which rests upon it to watch over the cradle of the race; to see that human beings are well born, well nourished, and well educated."[10]

Blackwell embraced that responsibility from the very beginnings of her career. She dedicated her life to improving the lives of her patients. She set the mark high for other women wanting an absorbing career in medicine. She was a trailblazer. Paths in medicine for women are well lit because of her efforts. She once wrote, "I knew that, however, insignificant my individual effort might be, it was in the right direction, and in accordance with . . . our [human] race's progress."[11] Her efforts exceeded her expectations. They were far from insignificant.

CHAPTER NOTES

INTRODUCTION. BLAZING TRAILS

1. Blackwell, Elizabeth, Classic Reprint Series, *Pioneer Work for Women* (London: Forgotten Books, 2015), p. 35.
2. Nancy Kline, *Elizabeth Blackwell: A Doctor's Triumph* (Berkeley, CA: Conari Press, 1997), p. xii.
3. Abram, Ruth J., *"Send Us a Lady Physician:"* Women Doctors in America, 1835–1920 (New York: W.W. Norton & Company, 1985), p. 64.

CHAPTER 1. BIRTH OF A WORLD CHANGER

1. Blackwell, Elizabeth, Classic Reprint Series, *Pioneer Work for Women* (London: Forgotten Books, 2015), p. 1.
2. LeClair, Mary K., Justin D. White, Susan Keeter, M.F.A., *Three 19th Century Women Doctors* (Syracuse, NY: Hoffman Press, 2007), p. 4.
3. Blackwell, p. 28.
4. Ibid., p. 1.
5. Ibid., p. 2.
6. Ibid.
7. Leclair, p. 5.
8. Ibid.
9. Shearer Benjamin F., and Barbara S. Shearer, *Medical Dictionary* (Westport, CT: 1996), p. 33.

10. Blackwell, p. 9.

CHAPTER 2. ROAD LESS TRAVELED

1. Blackwell, Elizabeth, Classic Reprint Series, *Pioneer Work for Women* (London: Forgotten Books, 2015), p. 21.
2. Ibid., p. 9.
3. Ibid.
4. Ibid., p. 11.
5. Ibid, p.16–17.
6. Baker, Jean H., *Sisters: The Lives of America's Suffragists* (New York: Hill and Wang, 2005), p. 13.
7. Blackwell, p. 21.
8. Ibid., p. 23.
9. Ibid., p. 50.
10. Ibid., p. 73

CHAPTER 3. COMPASSIONATE CARE

1. Blackwell, Elizabeth, Classic Reprint Series, *Pioneer Work for Women* (London: Forgotten Books, 2015), p. 51.
2. Ibid., p. 90.
3. Ibid., 145.
4. Ibid., p. 139.
5. Ibid., p. 153.
6. Ibid., p. 154.
7. Ibid., p. 157.

8. Ibid.
9. Ibid., p. 158.

CHAPTER 4. PARTNERS IN MEDICINE

1. Blackwell, Elizabeth, Classic Reprint Series, *Pioneer Work for Women* (London: Forgotten Books, 2015), p. 140.
2. Ibid., Appendix, Section, III, p. 234.
3. Ibid., p. 159.
4. Ibid., p. 162.
5. Ibid., p. 162.
6. Ibid., p. 163.
7. Ibid., p. ix.
8. Ibid., p. 143.
9. Ibid., p. 163.
10. Ibid., p. 160.

CHAPTER 5. WAR ON SICKNESS AND DISEASE

1. Blackwell, Elizabeth, Classic Reprint Series, *Pioneer Work for Women* (London: Forgotten Books, 2015), p. 160.
2. Ibid., p. 169.
3. Ibid., p. 145.
4. Ibid., p. 177.
5. Ibid., p. 189.
6. Blackwell, p. 190.

INDEX